THE BUTTERFLY CHRISTMAS

WILLIAM MCDONALD

First Edition: October 2022
printed in the United States of America
ISBN: 9798355191061

Cover Photo: iStock

Cover Design: Scott Woldin

❀ Created with Vellum

For everyone who still believes

READERS HAVE BEEN TOUCHED BY THE BUTTERFLY CHRISTMAS

I found myself completely immersed in this wonderful story. One word comes to mind. WOW! Totally blown away with the message of hope.
—Lenny/Newport Beach, California

It's beautifully written - not like any other Christmas story I've read - the message is lovely. —Valerie/Burlington, Ontario

The book is beautiful. I found myself taking notes of things that particularly moved me but had to stop because there were so many. This is all just divine. And, best of all, one (me) need not believe in a structured divinity to embrace it.
—Paty/Phoenix, Arizona

What an inspirational story! It seems like every word turns to gold and my heart turns to mush! —Peggy/Pleasant Prairie, Wisconsin

Marvelous! I love the message of hope spread throughout the pages.
—Betsy/Erie, Pennsylvania

I get something new each time I read it. There's something special in this story.
—Diane/Magalia, California

Beautiful, soulful, and tender. Simple, elegant, and heartfelt.
—Mari/Asheville, North Carolina

It's been too long since we've had a book like this. I cried, I enjoyed, I pondered, especially about the river in heaven.
—Candace/Hollywood, Florida

CHAPTER ONE

THE FIRST LETTER

DEAR SANTA CLAUS,

MOM SAYS YOU MIGHT NOT COME TO OUR HOUSE THIS YEAR BUT MY SISTER IS SICK SO WILL YOU PLEASE MAKE HER BETTER FROM THE NORTH POLE? THANK YOU, SANTA.

YOUR FRIEND,
DONNA WORTHY

CHAPTER TWO

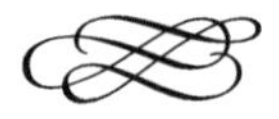

HEAVEN

"ARE YOU HERE, GOD?"

"I AM."

"I GOT THIS LETTER." Santa held Donna Worthy's letter up over his head for all of heaven to see.

"I'LL TAKE CARE OF IT."

"BUT SHE WROTE TO *ME*, GOD." Santa pulled Donna's letter to his chest. "She wants *me* to help."

"I'LL TAKE CARE OF IT."

. . .

"But ..."

"I'll take care of it."

CHAPTER THREE

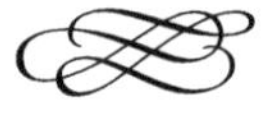

GRODAN

LIFE WENT ON.

CHRISTMAS WAS COMING.

GRODAN, the elder elf - some said he was a thousand years old, some said even older - with more power than any elf in the known and unknown worlds, and who saw what no one else could see, saw to it that warm meals found their way to men, women and children wondering when they would eat again; that a thick blanket and an extra bed somehow came available to a man, a woman or even a child wishing, hoping, praying for just one night in a bed not made of cardboard, under a blanket not made of newspaper; that a dollar or two would miraculously flutter into the path of the parent wondering where the next dollar would come from.

THE IMPOSSIBLE MADE POSSIBLE.

. . .

BUT THERE WAS A PROBLEM.

NOT GRODAN, not Santa, not his wife, whom everyone called "Mrs.", not a soul at the North Pole said it aloud but they all thought it, all knew it ... believing in the impossible was becoming something fewer and fewer people believed in.

A PROBLEM that was about to get impossibly worse than any of them could have imagined.

CHAPTER FOUR

THE SECOND LETTER

DEAR SANTA CLAUS,

MY SISTER DIED. I THOUGHT YOU WERE GOING TO MAKE HER BETTER.

YOUR FRIEND,
DONNA WORTHY

CHAPTER FIVE

HEAVEN

Heaven is a place of peace. Of love. Of comfort. And joy. And, on this particular day, tears.

"You said You'd take care of it God, and now she's gone." Santa raised both arms in surrender.

"She has not gone. She has gone on."

Old Saint Nick closed his eyes, bowed his head and whispered, "I should have done something."

He shook his head slowly back and forth.

"I should have done something." he whispered again.

He thought.

And thought.

And thought - and then suddenly opened his eyes.

"Maybe I still can."

CHAPTER SIX

THE NORTH POLE

"YOU DID WHAT?"

"I quit."

Mrs. Claus smiled, touched her husband's arm.

"You can't quit. You're Saint Nicholas, Kris Kringle, Father Christmas ... Santa Claus."

"Not any more." He waved Donna Worthy's letter in his wife's face, like a white flag. "Don't you understand what has happened here?"

"No, I don't understand and neither do you. But quitting who you are won't change what has happened. The only thing it will change is Christmas."

Santa touched her cheek. Gently. "Mrs., Christmas changed a long time ago."

"Not for the children."

He sighed, looked down at the letter in his hand.

"It did for this one. I have to find her. I have to explain."

"Explain what?" Mrs. snapped. "That you're not God?" She hesitated, her lips pressed tightly together, uncertain whether to say it or not. Decided to say it. "Or that you blame God?"

The silence hung in the air between them. He left it hanging, walked into the bathroom, came out an hour later looking nothing like the man who had gone in.

CHAPTER SEVEN

GOODBYE SANTA

GRODAN'S JAW DROPPED.

He has seen an Aigamuchab, the creature with eyes on the bottom of its feet. He has seen Golems, huge, human-like monsters made of wood, Sleipnir the eight-legged horse, gremlins, pesky little monsters with pointed ears, a unicorn and of course, flying reindeer.

But this?

"This is impossible!"

The elder elf blinked once, twice, three times, trying to unsee the impossible. The man who used to be Santa Claus ... gone. In his place a man whose hair had been hacked short, whose beard had been sheared to stubble and whose voice - a voice that had always sounded as happy as a children's choir - was now barely a whisper.

"I'm leaving, Grodan."

Even more impossible.

"Leaving? But Santa, what about Christmas?"

"That's not me anymore."

CHAPTER EIGHT

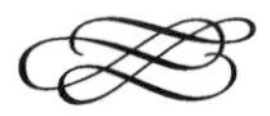

THE PARK

Late on a snowy Saturday afternoon, silent and still, Donna Worthy lay on her back, put her glasses on and tried to see into heaven. She didn't like to wear her glasses outside in the winter because they kept fogging up, making it impossible for her to see anything, but this was important. Maybe, with her glasses on, Donna might see Butterfly running, pain free, stirring up a heavenly breeze, scattering joy.

The snowflakes brushed softly against her face, the way her mother's hair did when she leaned down to kiss her goodnight.

A mocking-bird called. Butterfly would like that, Donna thought. Butterfly liked things with wings.

Especially butterflies.

Saturdays, Donna and Butterfly would sit with their father on one of the park benches and listen to him tell butterfly stories too impossible to be true.

"Close your eyes," he would say. "And hold out a hand."

Into each hand he would drop two rose petals.

"That's how much the Monarch butterfly weighs," he told them. "And yet its wings are so strong it can fly thousands of miles, as fast as the wind, as high as the clouds."

For the rest of that day, Butterfly called herself Monarch and ran, from room to room, as fast as the wind, as high as the clouds, even though every step she took in her thick, soft slippers felt to her like she was running barefoot over bits and pieces of broken glass.

And Butterfly's father would close his eyes and say, "Did a butterfly just flutter by?" and Butterfly would squeal with delight.

One Saturday, not long ago, their father told them that, according to legend, the arrival of the female Cabbage butterfly, white with two dark spots in the middle of her wing, is a sign that summer is coming right behind her. Butterfly went home, painted two big black splotches on a towel and flew around the house, singing, "Summer is coming right behind me! Summer is coming right behind me!"

It would be her last summer.

Again Donna looked up, hoping to see beyond the clouds, thick with snow, beyond the velvet sky, all the way into heaven.

But, even with her glasses on, she could not see all the way into heaven.

There was one thing she could do, though. Still lying in the snow, Donna slowly swished her arms and legs up and down, in and out, up and down, in and out again and again and then very carefully rose from her snowy bed, took a step back, looked down at the snow angel and then looked up.

"It's for you, Butterfly."

She watched her words drift into the sky on frozen breath.

And wished.

And wished.

And wished there were some way she could go with them.

Donna Worthy missed her sister. She missed the silliness that filled every room and every heart she was in. She missed her courage and her curiosity; she missed Saturdays in the park, gone now, tossed to the wind, like the down of a thistle.

Donna curled her arms tightly around herself and sent her lonely thoughts to the wishing stars just now beginning to nudge their way into the darkening sky.

A few moments slipped by, unnoticed. A few snowflakes tumbled into her hair, unnoticed.

Finally, she turned and shuffled slowly from the park, her heart in chains, not daring to look at the towering sycamore trees bending close to one another, like wooden giants, whispering secrets they knew about Donna Worthy and how it was her fault that Butterfly had died.

CHAPTER NINE

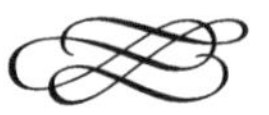

THE LIGHTHOUSE

It wasn't a secret, it was just something he had never shared with anyone.

On Christmas Eve, Santa liked to linger a little in a few of of his favorite spots around the world. One of those spots was the Presque Isle Lighthouse in Erie, Pennsylvania - Presque Isle coming from the French presqu'île, meaning "almost island". Santa never stayed longer than just long enough to breathe in the winter peace of a lake at rest beneath nearly three feet of ice; a silent peace, almost holy, like a host of angels holding its breath.

On this December day a few weeks before Christmas, the man who used to be Santa Claus stood at the top of the lighthouse tower, looked out over the frozen lake and felt no peace. Instead, he felt lost, alone, an almost person stranded on an almost island.

Behind him stood Erie, Pennsylvania, on the south shore of Lake Erie, three thousand, three hundred and eleven miles from the North Pole.

And home to Donna Worthy.

Tomorrow, he would find Donna Worthy. He would tell her that he had wanted to help her sister, had tried to help her sister, couldn't help her sister. He would explain ...

"Explain what? That you're not God? Or that you blame God?"

... and then he would leave and become who more and more people every year said he was ... an imaginary person living in an imaginary world.

The man who used to be Santa Claus touched his finger to his nose and went from the top of the lighthouse tower to the bottom, just by thinking it. He could still do that. He didn't know why because that was something only Santa Claus could do - travel

from wherever he was to wherever he wanted to be just by thinking it. But he wasn't Santa Claus anymore.

Not officially.

CHAPTER TEN

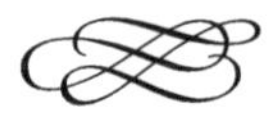

INSIDE DONNA WORTHY'S HOME

Not too far from the Presque Isle Lighthouse, in a warm, sweet-smelling home, Donna Worthy felt her mother's hair tickle her face as she leaned close to kiss her daughter goodnight.

"Were you in the park again today, Donna?"

A nod.

"Maybe one day you'll take me with you?"

Silence. Then, "Mom, do you miss Butterfly?"

She asked her mother the same question every night and every night her mother would close her eyes and remember ... tiny fingers, tiny toes, tiny nose - and a tiny blister on her new baby's heel, never suspecting what it might be.

Danni Worthy pressed her face next to Donna's, remembering the pain, the sorrow, the unspeakable; remembering Butterfly in her ultra-soft sheepskin pajamas, snuggling deep into her water mattress. She remembered Joe, her husband, poking his head into the room and saying, "Did a butterfly just flutter by?" And she remembered how Butterfly would squeal with delight. She remembered ...

"I'm going into my cocoon now, Mama, and when I wake up, I will be a butterfly."

How many times had Danni wished that she could be that cocoon for her daughter? How many times had she prayed that she could wrap herself around her Butterfly and protect her from what was to come?

"I miss her with all my heart," Danni whispered so softly her words barely moved the air around them. Opening her eyes, she added, "But we're going to make it, you and me and Dad, 'cause we're a bunch of tough old birds."

She smiled, kissed her daughter again and then stood and walked softly from the room. Donna waited a moment before leaning over the side of her bed, reaching under it and pulling out a box of colored pens and a large sketch pad. Turning to a clean sheet of paper, she began to draw.

The drawing looked like all the others in the sketch pad. Pictures she had drawn every night since Butterfly had died. Pictures of a girl. A girl with wings. Butterfly wings.

Outside, it was snowing. Flakes as thick and as soft as Butterfly's winter socks.

CHAPTER ELEVEN

OUTSIDE DONNA WORTHY'S HOME

NO ONE SAW HIM. NO ONE COULD. WITH THE EARLY NIGHTFALL AND the driving snow, only moments ago soft and thick, like Butterfly's winter socks, now sharp and cutting, like the pain Butterfly felt with every step she took, anyone could walk right past the man in red and not realize he was there. He wondered himself. Why *was* he here, on the street where Donna Worthy lived? To help shoulder the burden of pain a young girl was trying to carry alone? Or was he here to add to his own burden of guilt?

THERE WAS a mall not far from where the man who used to be Santa Claus stood. He would go there. Sit. Think. Decide what he was going to say to Donna Worthy when he knocked at her door the next morning.

CHAPTER TWELVE

THE MALL

THE MALL WAS DRESSED IN ITS CHRISTMAS BEST. TWO MILLION TWO hundred thousand square feet of indoor winter wonderland alive with music and magic and ribbons and bows and even mistletoe hanging over the door of a candy store advertising chocolate Christmas kisses. Thousands of giant dancing snowflakes waltzed their way gently back and forth across the ceiling, like debutantes dressed in all the colors of Christmas. And there were lights. More lights than the man who used to be Santa Claus had ever seen in the same place at the same time. A sign next to the bench he was seated on boasted that it had taken three thousand, three hundred man hours just to get those lights just right. In the middle of it all, holiday shoppers hurrying here, there and everywhere. Nothing and no one was standing still.

Except for the fellow who plopped down like a bag of water onto the bench next to old Saint Nicholas.

He was wide, not tall, beefy not bulky and his neck was as thick and as round as a bowling ball. Bushy white eyebrows crawled over his tired eyes like a pair of caterpillars trying to inch their way down to a nose as big as a beet and as red as a stop sign. A beard that wasn't really a beard dangled by a string from one ear.

And he was dressed up like Santa Claus.

"Yer gonna need this," he said, yanking the fake beard from his face and handing it over to the man who used to be Santa Claus.

"Why would I need that?"

"Well, yer suit looks pretty legit and you can cover that lousy haircut with the Santa hat but them kids won't buy that face without a beard so here, take it, it's on the house, I don't need it anymore 'cause I just quit."

"You quit?"

"Yeah, the money's good but it ain't easy. I gotta quit before them kids eat me alive."

"Quit?"

"Bein' Santa Claus. I quit bein' Santa. Imagine that," he finger wrote into the air, "Santa Claus Quits'. Ain't that a headline?"

He chuckled, quietly to himself, like someone enjoying a private joke, then louder and then even louder until the chuckling became a silly, almost hysterical laughter.

The man who used to be Santa Claus jumped up from the bench like he'd been sitting on fire and ran.

"Hey, where ya goin? Come back!"

He did not come back. He ran.

And ran.

And ran like he was running from the Ghost of Christmas Past. And then he stumbled, and tumbled, face-first into a green velvet, high-backed throne sitting empty on a raised platform next to the sign:

MEET SANTA!

Daily 9 AM - Noon
1PM-5PM

CHAPTER THIRTEEN

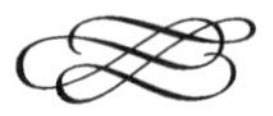

THE BOGEYMAN

THE MAN WHO USED TO BE SANTA CLAUS OPENED HIS EYES, SHOOK HIS head, tried to stand, fell back down.

"Whoa, ease up there, Santa, you just took a knock-out punch."

The old saint squinted up at the odd creature looking down at him. His voice sounded like someone walking on frozen snow.

"I'm not Santa. Who are you and why are you calling me Santa?"

"I'm the Bogeyman."

His face seemed to be shrinking, collapsing into itself. One ear appeared normal, the other almost miniature, sticking out from the side of his head like a flag. He had tufts of hair sprouting here and there around patches of bald scalp, like water lilies on a pond and one of his eyebrows had a beginning and an end but no middle.

"You're the Bogeyman?"

"That's me. The guy in the back of the room. The guy nobody looks at but if they do they wished they never did. That's who *I* am, okay? An' I know *you're* not Santa. Not the real one, anyway, but hey ... the red suit ... I just figured you for one of them mall Santas."

Again, the man who used to be Santa Claus tried to stand, took a few wobbly steps backward and fell, this time onto the green velvet throne. Still dizzy, he glanced toward the food court, hoping not to see the Ghost of Christmas Past, losing hope as he saw him rumbling toward the throne, waving his fake beard in the air.

Sandwiched between the Bogeyman and the Ghost of Christmas past, the man who used to be Santa Claus could think of only one thing to do.

He touched his finger to his nose and disappeared.

CHAPTER FOURTEEN

THE LIGHTHOUSE

He didn't know where else to go. Back to the street where Donna Worthy lived? Not tonight. Back to the North Pole? To do what? So he came here, to the lighthouse. It was safe. Quiet. Closed for the winter.

"Like you," he mouthed to his own red reflection in the window.

A reflection he no longer recognized. For as long as he could remember he had been Santa Claus, the keeper of Christmas, bringing joy to every girl and boy who still believed. One of them, a girl named Donna Worthy, had reached out to him, begged him to help, believed he could help, never doubted he *would* help.

I'll take care of it.

God had promised. God would take care of it. That was what He did - took care of things - so Santa went back to doing what *he* did - making lists and checking them twice, sorting the names into naughty and nice. Life at the North Pole went on.

In Erie, Pennsylvania, a child's life ended.

God *didn't* take care of it; didn't do His job. A sister lost a sister. A mother and father lost a daughter.

And Santa Claus lost what had always kept him believing.

Faith.

"You quit." he mouthed again to the sad red reflection in the window. "Ain't that a headline?"

Turning away, the old saint began to pace back and forth across the lighthouse floor, slowly, heavily, like a man dragging a bag of troubles behind him. Finally, he leaned against the wall, slid to the floor, closed his eyes and troubled himself to sleep.

CHAPTER FIFTEEN

DANNI WORTHY

DANNI WORTHY WAS SHOVELING SNOW.

"I can help you with that."

She looked up. Couldn't help but smile at what she saw.

"No offense, mister, but you look like Santa Claus on a bad hair day after a rough night."

It *had* been a rough night for the man who used to be Santa Claus. Not long after he had troubled himself to sleep, he troubled himself awake. And then asleep again and then awake again. And again and again and again all long night long.

Awkwardly running his hand through his cropped hair, the man who used to be Santa Claus smiled back at Danni Worthy and said, "I'm not Santa Claus. Just a guy with a bad haircut. But I can help you with the shoveling." He lifted the shovel he was carrying into the air, like a trophy. "Got my own shovel."

The shovel, propped against the lighthouse door had given him an idea and now here he was, face-to-face with the woman he assumed, hoped was Donna Worthy's mother.

She smiled again. A tired smile, he thought.

"I'd love the help but we can't afford it right now. Thank you, though." She bent over her shovel, pushed some snow from the walk, grunted as she said, "My husband usually does this but he's down with some sort of bug ." She tried to lift the shovel, grunted again, tried again.

Old Saint Nick watched her struggle under the weight of the snow, stepped forward and gently touched her on the shoulder.

"There's no charge."

She looked up at him, studied him, tilted her head.

"No charge? Seriously?"

"Seriously."

She studied him again, a little more closely. At first glance just a harmless looking round-bellied guy with a bad haircut walking around in a Santa suit. There was something else, though. She didn't know what but ... something.

"Shovel all this snow for nothing? Why would you do that?"

"If it'll make you feel better, I'll shovel the sidewalk and the driveway in return for a cup of hot chocolate and a cookie. I really like cookies."

"'Course you like cookies, you're Santa Claus." She smiled again, this time brightly, and added, "On a bad hair day."

"So, deal?"

"Deal. Have at it."

She drove her shovel into the snow, like someone planting a flag in a new world, turned and climbed the steps to her front door, stopped, turned to face him again.

"Christmas spirit."

"Excuse me?"

"Christmas spirit," she said again. "Nice to see it's still alive in some people."

Before he could answer, Danni Worthy turned and disappeared inside her house.

CHAPTER SIXTEEN

A SIMPLE PLAN

It was a simple plan. He'd shovel the sidewalk and the driveway, she'd come out to say thank you with hot chocolate and cookies, he'd tell her he really was Santa Claus but not anymore and if he could have just a few minutes with her daughter, he'd be on his way.

He shoveled the sidewalk and the driveway, shoveled it again after the snow plow went by and was just finishing when Danni Worthy came out of the house holding a mug of steaming hot chocolate in one hand, a plate of cookies and a napkin in the other, placing it all on top of a trash bin parked next to the garage.

"You can leave the plate and the mug on the doorstep and toss the napkin in the trash bin and ..." She folded her hands together in front of her like she was praying. ".... thank you, thank you, thank you? You never did tell me your name."

. . .

He smiled.

"Believe it or not, my real name is ..."

"Santa!"

A voice thundered behind him, a heavy hand clamped down on his shoulder and spun him around.

CHAPTER SEVENTEEN

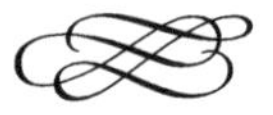

ROGER

The man who used to be Santa Claus found himself looking up.

And up.

And up, into the face of a giant - a man who, if he wasn't seven feet tall, was close enough to it to lie about it. He had thick black hair, pulled into a ponytail, a nose and jaw so sharp they could cut glass and midnight blue eyes that shone with the intensity of a mind reader. He wore a thick, camel-colored coat and smooth leather matching gloves.

"Nice gimmick with the Santa suit, pal, and hey, it works for me! My lucky day, your lucky day!" the giant bellowed. "Here I am, on my way out and bam! there comes the snow plow pushing a mountain of snow right back into the driveway! Who's got time to deal with that? I'm asking myself and bam! there you are. My lucky day, your lucky day! Clear what that plow dumped at the end of my driveway, make yourself a fast forty and ..." He shoved two twenty dollar bills into the old saint's hand "... get a haircut." He winked and lumbered away.

"Wow, Santa, forty dollars! Like a little Christmas miracle" Danni Worthy said with a smile. "Good ol' Roger."

"Roger?"

"Our neighbor. Roger."

"He's very ... abrupt."

She smiled, cocked her head in the direction the big man had walked off. "Yep, that's Roger. Mister Abrupt." Her smile warmed. "But he's really just a big ol' teddy bear." She clapped her hands. "Better let you get to it." She turned and was back in the house before the man in the Santa suit could say another word. With a sigh, he shoved the bills into his pocket, took a sip of hot chocolate, a bite out of a cookie - oatmeal raisin, one of his favorites - and then walked to the end of the big man's driveway and began to shovel. Minutes later, the garage door opened, the big man, driving a big car, tore down the driveway and onto the street, honked, waved a gloved hand out the window, honked again and drove off.

The hot chocolate had cooled. He finished it anyway, along with the half-eaten oatmeal raisin cookie. Sticking the rest of the cookies into his pocket, he wadded the napkin into a ball and lifted the lid to the trash bin. The book was the first thing he saw.

All About Butterflies

It hadn't been tossed into the trash bin. It had been placed there, like a sacred thing. Like an unanswered prayer.

The man who used to be Santa Claus lifted the book from the trash can, opened it, looked around to be sure no one was watching.

Someone was.

CHAPTER EIGHTEEN

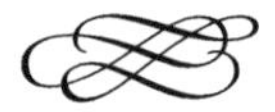

MAE ROSE

She was old and full of years. Maybe ninety, maybe more if you could read between the lines on her face.

"Does Danni know you're digging through her trash?"

Her voice crackled and wheezed, like wet twigs in a fire as she picked her way slowly, carefully up the driveway, toward the man who used to be Santa Claus. She wore a faded pink terry cloth robe, black rubber boots and a pink knitted cap pulled tight over hair as white as cotton, as thin as thread.

"Danni?" Santa asked.

The old woman pointed at the house. "My neighbor, Danielle Worthy. Folks around here call her Danni. Does she know you're digging through her trash?"

"Well, I wasn't really digging, I ..." He held up the book. "I was reading."

"Nothing to be ashamed of, mister, digging through the trash, being hungry. Me and Franklin, my husband, God rest his soul, we went through some hungry times. We weren't ashamed. Just hungry. Name's Mae Rose. Come on across, we'll have soup."

She turned and started inching her way back down the driveway in the direction of a small, cottage style house on the other side of the street. "Bring your shovel," she called over her shoulder. "Snow's deeper than it looks."

Tucking *All About Butterflies* into his pocket, the old saint grabbed his shovel and followed Mae Rose across the street.

"You clear a pathway and I'll put the soup on. Don't worry about the driveway. There's a car in the garage but the tires are flat and Franklin, God rest his soul, is gone and my driving days gone with him so ..." She shrugged, smiled weakly.

The man who used to be Santa Claus smiled back, just as weakly, nodded his head, lowered his shovel and quickly cleared enough of a path to get Mae Rose safely to her front door.

The old girl disappeared into the house. The old saint stood, for a few minutes, looking back across the street at the house where Donna Worthy lived. He'd go back, knock on the door and ...

"Soup's on!"

Still wearing the faded pink terry cloth robe and pink knitted cap and now holding a bony gray cat, Mae Rose stood on the doorstep waving him in.

"Hurry, now, it's not going to eat itself."

CHAPTER NINETEEN

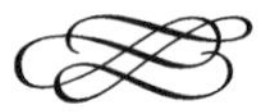

GRODAN

GRODAN STOOD LOOKING UP AT WHAT ONLY HE COULD SEE - HUMA THE compassionate bird of good fortune and joy, living its entire life flying invisibly high above the earth. There was so little joy at the North Pole since Santa had left that Grodan dared wonder if perhaps the great bird had been sent directly to him on the wings of hope?

HE COULD ONLY HOPE.

MRS. CLAUS REFUSED TO DESPAIR. Her husband had left. Her husband would return. "He is too full of goodness and giving. It is impossible for him to walk away."

BUT SANTA *HAD* WALKED AWAY and Grodan, who could see into tomorrow and beyond, could not see his friend on any coming horizon.

. . .

He looked again to the sky, saw the snow white Caladrius bird, known for taking the sickness and grief of others upon itself.

"Can you take our grief upon your wings?" the old elf called to the white bird.

He could only hope.

CHAPTER TWENTY

FRANKLIN, BUTTERFLY AND SOUP

MAE ROSE WATCHED THE OLD FELLOW EAT THE SOUP; WATCHED TILL SHE cried.

"Franklin, God rest his soul, used to eat like that."

The man who used to be Santa Claus looked up. Waited.

"I'd put a bowl of my soup down in front of him and he would look at me every time like I was the queen of the world and he would eat my soup every time like he was the king of the world. He always said eating my soup was like eating dessert and then he would say, 'Only the pure in heart can make a good soup.' You know who said that, mister? Beethoven said that. Imagine, him being so busy with all that music of his, taking the time to talk about soup."

"Maybe he had a Mae Rose of his own?"

She smiled. "My Franklin got the Alzheimer's. Got to the point where he couldn't tell the difference between a fork and a spoon."

She paused, shook her head sadly and almost whispered, "And soup."

Mae Rose turned to face the man who used to be Santa Claus.

"If Franklin could have seen himself at the end, not knowing who he was, who I was ... what soup was ... I think he would've said 'I have to go now, Mae" and I think that's why God took him, so he could be himself again. 'Course then I have to wonder why He let him get the Alzheimer's in the first place." She turned back to the window, looked at the house across the street. "And the Butterfly. I wonder about her, too."

"The butterfly?"

"Danni's youngest. They called her Butterfly."

He touched the book in his pocket. *All About Butterflies.*

"She was a pretty thing, always happy, always running around flapping those make-believe wings of hers like she was a real butterfly. You'd never know she had that awful skin disease. You can't imagine the pain she had to put up with."

She turned to face him again.

"It's hard to lose someone. Doesn't matter if it's someone who doesn't know who they are anymore or someone who never got to find out who they were going to be. It's hard."

The old saint bowed his head, stared into the soup bowl in front of him. Didn't feel hungry anymore.

"The Butterfly's sister, Donna, took it hard. Don't see her much anymore and even when she does come out of the house, she spends all her time alone in the park."

He lifted his head. "The park?"

"Yes," she pointed to her left. "A couple of blocks over."

He stared in the direction she was pointing, his mind working, his eyebrows slowly raising. Mae Rose snapped her fingers.

"Eat your soup."

CHAPTER TWENTY-ONE

THE PARK

MAE ROSE TURNED THE TALK TO MEMORIES OF EASIER TIMES, EASIER days. The old saint managed his way through another bowl of creamy carrot soup before pushing himself away from the table, patting his round belly and saying he was going to have to go walk it off.

SHE WALKED him to the door, still carrying the bony gray cat.

"THINGS'LL GET BETTER FOR YOU." She said it like it was a promise. "You just have to believe."

HE MANAGED A FEEBLE SMILE, thanked her again for the soup. "It made me feel like the king of the world," he said with a more genuine smile and stepped outside.

"MORE SNOW COMING," he thought, looking skyward. He was right. Winter in this part of the country was a season of mood swings, and the pendulum could swing without warning. A gentle snowfall one moment was a vicious storm the next. Mood swings.

STEALING a quick glance across the street at Donna Worthy's house, the man in the red suit turned left and walked in the direction of the park.

~

It was not a big park, it looked more to the old saint like the friendly neighborhood park at the end of the street. Dogwoods, hemlocks, sycamores, pines, maples, they were all there, in groups or scattered haphazardly along one of the three pathways that led in and out of the park. The maples, shaped like upside down ice-cream cones, were especially elegant, covered in frost, looking like crystal clad divas on their way to the winter ball. A few red cardinals lunched on the drupes of the dogwood while a noisy band of mockingbirds and warblers waited impatiently out of sight in the evergreens for their share of the leftovers.

The sleepy little park seemed to be calling to the man who used to be Santa Claus, inviting him, almost pulling him into the quiet.

"Not today." he said. "I have an idea."

Touching his finger to his nose, he imagined himself back at the lighthouse, and went there, staying only long enough to return the shovel to where he had found it. Touching his finger to his nose once again, he imagined himself back at the mall, and went there.

CHAPTER TWENTY-TWO

THE INVISIBLE MAN

THE MAN WHO USED TO BE SANTA CLAUS SETTLED INTO A QUIET SPOT IN the back of the food court and began to read *All About Butterflies ... Worldwide, we have found approximately 20,000 species of butterflies, about 725 of them in North America and...*

"Is that you?'

It was the Bogeyman, standing a few feet away from the old saint, cautiously poking him with a walking stick, like he would poke a sleeping snake.

"Don't do that!"

The Bogeyman kept doing it.

"Don't do that!" The old saint swatted at the stick.

The Bogeyman leaned in and half-whispered, "Just testing, Santa. Or should I say ..." he looked around again, added, surreptitiously, "... The Invisible Man?"

"Stop calling me Santa," He yanked the stick from the Bogeyman's hand. "Invisible man?"

The Bogeyman dragged a chair close to the man who used to be Santa Claus, sat and looked around, like someone being followed, before looking back at the old saint, squinting and, still whispering, "Last time I saw you, you were there and then poof!" He lifted both hands into the air. "You were gone. Disappeared. E-vap-o-rated.." He raised his eyebrows.

"You were just seeing things."

"I *was* seein' things, and then I *wasn't* seein' those same things! Come on, what's goin' on? You can tell me. I believe in that stuff."

"Stuff?"

"Yeah, you know ... stuff. Like invisible people an' magic an' luck an' ESP an' even Santa Claus. No offense but even with the red suit, you still ain't him."

"Then stop calling me him."

"No problem. What should I call you?"

"Nick," he said without hesitation. "Call me Nick."

"Okay, Nick. Nick, the invisible man."

CHAPTER TWENTY-THREE

LENNY SCHWARTZ

NICK SPENT A LITTLE MORE THAN HALF OF ONE OF THE TWENTY DOLLAR bills Roger had given him on a couple of Philly Cheesesteaks from a place called Charleys.

"If you can't make it to Philly, make it to Charleys," the Bogeyman said, holding his sandwich up to his nose and inhaling. Closing his eyes he added, "If this right here ain't a piece of art, it's a work of art! Almost hate to take a bite." He took a bite. "Almost." He grinned. "So, Nick, you gonna tell me who you really are? Like if you're from another planet or somethin'."

"I'm not from another planet, I'm from another place and if you want to believe you saw me disappear, I can't stop you."

"'Course I believe it. I *saw* it. At first I thought you might be a ghost. That's why I was pokin' you - to see if my stick would go right through you. I believe in ghosts but I'm glad you're not one."

"I'm not a ghost. I'm just an ordinary man here to visit a friend and when our visit is over, I'll just dis ... be on my way."

The Bogeyman nodded and pointed his cheesesteak at the book on the table..

"What's with the butterflies?"

"I don't know." Nick stared down at the book, moved his hand slowly back and forth across its cover. "It's got something to do with why I'm here but ... I don't know." He looked over at the Bogeyman, changed the subject.

"So, you believe in ... stuff?"

"Yeah."

"Invisible people?"

"Yeah."

"Have you ever seen one?"

"I'm lookin' at one."

"Santa Claus?"

"'Yep."

"Have you ever seen him?"

"Nope."

"God?"

"'Course."

"Have you ever seen Him?"

"Nope."

"So you believe in what you've never seen?"

The Bogeyman set his cheesesteak aside and moved a little closer to Nick.

"Take a look at my face."

He did. He saw a face that appeared to be shrinking, collapsing into itself, an unusual eyebrow with a beginning and an end but no middle, a miniature ear sticking out from the side of his head like a flag and tufts of hair sprouting here and there around patches of bald scalp, like water lilies on a pink pond.

"The ugly duckling, right? Beauty and the Beast, right? The Bogeyman, right? Wrong. None of them is me. I'm Lenny Schwartz. I like dogs, I like baseball, I like walkin' in the snow, I like lookin' at the stars, I like ..." he tapped a finger on the book on the table. "... books and I like Charleys Philly Cheesesteaks."

He paused, leaned back in his chair.

"But who knows that, Nick? People look at me and nobody says, 'How ya doin'? How's yer day?' They don't see Lenny Schwartz. Lenny Schwartz is invisible to them. They see the Bogeyman, the poor slob with the ugly mug.

"So, yeah, Nick, I believe in what I can't see and I believe in what *they* can't see." He pointed to everyone in the food court. "Which happens to be the real me. Hey, maybe Lenny Schwartz is the *real* Invisible Man?"

The silence hung in the air between them like an unanswered question.

"Where you stayin', Nick?"

Nick straightened in his chair, a confused look on his face.

"I don't know."

Lenny stood and grabbed his walking stick.

"C'mom. I got a place."

CHAPTER TWENTY-FOUR

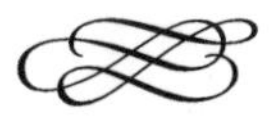

THE NORTH POLE

MRS. CLAUS STOOD ON THE PORCH WITH HER EYES CLOSED, HOPING that when she opened them she'd see Santa walking toward her, hear his familiar greeting, "Hello, Mrs., you're looking more than special today," always followed by a kiss and a look that said more than a thousand I love you's.

"COME HOME, SANTA," she said softly before turning and going back into their home, wiping her eyes with the corner of her apron, still not opening them.

CHAPTER TWENTY-FIVE

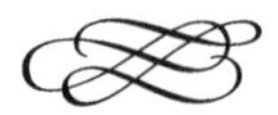

ST. PATRICK'S HAVEN

LENNY'S "PLACE" WAS ST. PATRICK'S HAVEN, A HOMELESS SHELTER FOR men, about five or six miles from the mall. It wasn't big, room for only twenty-four men, but it was warm. And welcoming. Like a light in the window. There was a clean bed and a hot shower for every man and the coffee was always fresh, always hot, always on.

"All the comforts of home, right Nick?" Lenny said, pouring himself a cup of coffee. "And real coffee mugs," he added, holding up his mug, like a trophy. "Kinda makes me feel like I'm a somebody." He sipped his coffee. "They got hot water too, Nick, in case you wanna make up some of them noodles in a cup."

Nick didn't answer. He had wandered down a hallway and into what was called the TV Room, where a group of men were watching a Christmas movie. A girl in the movie, dressed like an elf, was decorating a Christmas tree. Nick moved closer, closed his eyes and breathed in deeply.

"Like a walk in the forest," he whispered to himself.

One of the group watching the movie was a curly-haired redhead, no more than twenty years old.

"I used to do that with my Moms. It was good times." the redhead said to the man seated next to him.

"If it was so good, what're you doing here?"

The redhead didn't answer. Instead, he stood up, put his head down and turned away, bumping into Nick who had been inching closer and closer to the television.

"Sorry, citizen," he mumbled, patting Nick softly on the shoulder. "Hey," looking at the red suit, "Anyone ever tell you you look like Santa Claus?"

Still with his eyes locked on the television, Nick murmured, "I used to be Santa Claus."

The redhead laughed and gave Nick another, more solid pat on the shoulder. "Good one, citizen."

Nick's eyes remained locked on the television. On the girl dressed like an elf, decorating a Christmas tree.

CHAPTER TWENTY-SIX

THE TREE

THE CHRISTMAS TREE IN SANTA'S HOUSE HAD TO BE A SCOTCH PINE.

"Because you can stand next to it, close your eyes and breathe in the aroma of a walk in the forest," Santa always said and he was always right.

Decorating the big pine began with the smaller elves; small enough to fit into the palm of Santa's hand. Their assignment was to light the tree from the inside out. They would walk along the pine branches to the trunk of the tree and wrap a string of lights from its top to its bottom. That done, they would walk back across every branch, wrapping lights as they went, until the tree was completely lit.

Next, the bigger elves, some of them as tall as seven feet, would hang balls of all shapes, sizes and colors, one and only one on the tip of each branch, allowing the lights inside the tree to give them a mystic radiance.

Mrs. blew bubbles from the Bubble Jar. Hundreds of them, each one a different color. Bubbles so tiny they could fit through the eye of a needle. Bubbles that would float up, down, in and around the tree, bouncing from branch to branch, never popping, never stopping until the end of the twelfth day of Christmas.

Grodan, the elder elf, placed his annual gift beneath the tree. The gift of insight, wrapped in a small red box. At a specific time, and it is never the same time twice, but always no later than Christmas Eve, the small red box disappears from beneath the Scotch Pine in Santa's house and reappears in the hands of someone somewhere in the world. Someone who needs insight. Inside the red box is a mirror. When the person holding the mirror looks into it, they will see what they have been blinded to for far too long.

Santa was the last to touch the tree. He chose four branches; one facing east, one facing west, another north and another facing south. To each he attached a Star of Bethlehem flower symbolizing purity, honesty, innocence and hope.

"A compass for anyone losing their way," he would say.

A fifth Star of Bethlehem, representing forgiveness, was set on the ground next to Grodan's red box.

"For all who believe."

And then the old saint, Mrs. and all the elves would form a circle around the tree, hold hands, close their eyes, pray for a happy Christmas and breathe in the aroma of the Scotch Pine.

A walk in the forest.

CHAPTER TWENTY-SEVEN

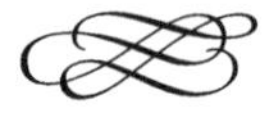

BETSY

"ONE OF MY FAVORITES."

Nick turned toward the voice; saw a woman standing next to him.

"The movie." She nodded in the direction of the TV. "It's *Elf,* one of my favorite Christmas movies. Right up there with *Christmas Vacation.* Hi!" she stuck out her hand. "I'm Betsy."

She had a smile that could light a candle and, behind her glasses, soft brown eyes as warm as a summer Sunday morning. Nick shook her hand, felt the strength of her grip.

"I'm Nick."

"Welcome, Nick. If you have any questions or if you feel like talking ... about the weather, about life ..." she angled her head toward the TV. " ... about movies, about anything, there are always a couple of men here who are good listeners. Or there's *me* and ..." she flashed a mischievous smile and held up a paper bag. "I bring bananas!"

Returning her smile, Nick said, "Thank you, Betsy, but I think tonight I'd just like to find a quiet corner and read my book."

"Not a problem. I'll be around for a little bit longer in case you feel like talking ... about books."

"Do I get a banana even if I'm just reading?"

She smiled that smile again, opened her paper bag, pulled out a banana and handed it to the old saint. "You get a banana just for being here."

NICK FOUND his quiet corner and then sat and nibbled on his banana, ate the rest of the oatmeal raisin cookies Danni Worthy had given him and read *All About Butterflies.* He learned that butterfly wings are transparent, that butterflies taste with their feet and live on an all-liquid diet; he learned that butterflies are nearsighted but they can see and discriminate colors and he learned that butterflies drink the tears of ...

"Pssst! Nick! C'mon, we gotta go!"

It was Lenny.

"Go where? Why are you whispering?"

"'Cause it's sack time. You an' me are the last two men standin' an' it's Lights Out around here at eleven. C'mon, the bedroom's this way."

The bedroom was one of four, each housing three bunkbeds. Nick settled into a bottom bunk just as the lights went out.

Lenny?" he whispered into the dark.

"Yo."

"Did you know butterflies drink tears?"

"Humph. who knew?"

WHILE NICK and Lenny and the men of St. Patrick's Haven were settling in for the night, four thousand and eighty-eight miles toward the other side of the world, in the city of Bern, one of the oldest clocks in Switzerland chimed seven in the morning. Feeling as old as the clock, Professor Mathias Pedersen sat on the edge of his bed, his down comforter wrapped around him like a cape, his legs stretched out before him, his toes wiggling.

"Today's the day."

He had been saying it every morning for months. Would today be the day? Donna Worthy's father's life depended on it.

CHAPTER TWENTY-EIGHT

THE PARK

DONNA WORTHY WAS AWAKE. HER MOTHER WAS NOT. HER FATHER was not.

They would have been awake if Butterfly were still here. They would have been changing the miles of bandages that seemed to be the only thing holding Butterfly together. It would take hours and they would have to do it all over again at bedtime.

Donna pulled on her boots and coat and scarf and mittens and left the house. She would go to the park, where she felt closest to Butterfly. There were no bandages there.

There was snow. Snow so deep it came almost to the top of her knees. She trudged her way to her favorite spot in the park and lay on her back and called into heaven.

"Are you an angel now, Butterfly?"

She didn't know if children got to be angels when they went to heaven but the thought was comforting because Butterfly had always wished she could have real wings and angels had wings, didn't they?

"If you *are* an angel, maybe you could fly down and see us? Daddy's sick right now, but if you came to see him, I bet it would make him feel better."

She waited for the answer that would not come, waited for the angel that would not come, waited for Butterfly, who would not come. Finally, she swished her arms and legs up and down, in and out, up and down, in and out and then carefully rose from her snowy bed, took a step back, looked down at the snow angel and then looked up.

"It's for you, Butterfly."

"It's perfect," came a voice from behind Donna.

She spun around, startled, to see a man sitting on the bench; an old man wearing what looked like a suit Santa Claus would wear.

"Really, it's a perfect snow angel. Best I've ever seen."

"It's not a snow angel, it's a Butterfly angel."

The old man said nothing. Didn't move from the bench.

"It's for my sister. Her name is Butterfly and she's in heaven and I make Butterfly angels for her so she knows I still come here even if she can't anymore."

"Did she used to come here?"

"We both did, with our dad, and we always sat on that bench where you are and he always brought his book and told us stories about butterflies."

All About Butterflies.

"I have to go." Donna said.

The child hurried off. When she reached the edge of the park, she turned and sent a shy wave toward the old man.

Nick smiled and waved back.

CHAPTER TWENTY-NINE

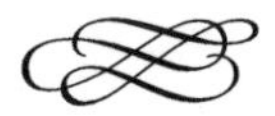

BUTTERFLY ANGELS

MONDAY, AFTER SCHOOL.

The minute Donna Worthy walked into the park, she saw them.

Butterfly angels.

Everywhere there was snow, there was a Butterfly angel.

"Do you like them?" she heard someone say in a voice as soft as air. It was the same old man she had met the day before, sitting on the same bench.

"Did you make them?" Donna asked.

"I did."

"All of them?"

"Every one."

"How many did you make?"

"A Kaleidoscope. Did you know that's what they call a group of butterflies?"

"No, but my Dad probably does."

"Probably, and he probably knows that sometimes a group of butterflies is also called a flutter."

An awkward silence nudged its way between them, separating them for a few minutes before the old man said, "My name is Nick."

She studied the old saint, tilting her head from side to side. "You look kinda like what Santa Claus would look if he didn't have a beard and long hair."

"Have you ever met Santa Claus?"

"Only at the mall. But mostly everybody knows that's not the real Santa 'cause when he whispers in your ear you can smell cigarette smoke on him. The *real* Santa Claus doesn't smell like cigarette smoke, so he's probably just there to listen and get messages."

"Messages?"

"Uh-huh. He listens to what all the kids tell him and then he writes it all down and puts it in a box and an elf comes and gets the box after the mall closes and he takes it to the real Santa."

"So you still believe in Santa Claus?"

She hesitated before answering. "Most of the time."

The awkward silence once again nudged its way between them, separating them until the young girl quietly said, "I have to go."

She turned quickly and walked away. Nick called after her.

"Donna Worthy, did you know that butterflies drink tear drops?"

She stopped. Didn't turn around.

"How do you know that?"

"I read it in a book about butterflies."

She nodded and then walked on toward home, not daring to ask her second question.

How do you know my name?

DANNI WORTHY STOOD on her front porch and watched her daughter, almost a shadow in the thickening snow, walk slowly toward home, head down, spirit down.

"She is a shadow," Danni thought. "A little lost shadow."

"Do you believe this?!"

It was Roger, standing in his driveway, knee-deep in snow.

"Gonna take forever to shovel this! Who's got time for that? Where's Santa when you need him?"

CHAPTER THIRTY

DANIEL

NICK WAS SITTING, EYES CLOSED, IN A SOUP KITCHEN NOT FAR FROM ST. Patrick's Haven. He had been welcomed here like an old friend but if he could be where he really wanted to be right now, he'd be in the park with Donna Worthy, making Butterfly angels, telling her who he really was and why he was here, in Erie, Pennsylvania. Telling her how sorry he was that Butterfly was gone. Trying to tell her it wasn't his fault. Trying to tell her ... what? That he wished ...

"Room for one more, citizen?"

Nick's eyes snapped open. Sliding into the seat opposite him was the redheaded kid he'd bumped into his first night at St Patrick's Haven.

"Good grub here," the kid said, picking up his fork. "Not good like my Moms used to make, but still good. Especially when you're hungry."

"How old are you?" Nick asked the redhead.

"Huh?" The kid looked at Nick, said nothing.

"I mean, you seem too young to be ... here?"

The redhead pointed with his fork toward a table where a mother, father and two young children sat eating, not looking up, not looking around, not wanting to be seen.

"Everybody's too young to be here." He looked at Nick. "Nobody asked to be here. Nobody wants to be here. But here we are, right? Citizens of the sidewalk. That's what I call us. I'm Citizen Daniel, by the way."

He stuck out a hand. Nick shook it. Soft hands, he thought.

Daniel seemed too young to know what he knew, to say what he said, but he was right. One day you're in your own home, living a good life and then, one missed paycheck, one wrong decision, one bad choice and you don't live there anymore. You live in a park, on a bench, under an overpass, in a car, a storage locker, trying to survive on the same streets you once took for granted. The people, the street people you might once have looked down on or looked away from, you now look to for help because they're suddenly someone you have too much in common with. They are your new family. You're an outcast, you're always tired, always hungry, always hiding.

"You staying at the Haven again tonight?" Daniel asked Nick.

"I am. Do you know if Lenny will be there? I didn't see him at sign-in."

"I don't know any Lenny."

Nick described him.

"Oh, you mean the Bogeyman! He's over there." Daniel lifted his chin toward a table near the window. "With the Pear Lady."

"The Pear Lady?"

"Uh-huh, she sells Christmas pears outside the mall."

Nick tried not to stare at the woman but he couldn't stop himself. She had a look about her. She might have been beautiful once. It was hard to tell. Her face was not especially dirty but not especially clean. Her hair, some gray, some blond, awkwardly covered one eye but there was no masking the sadness, the defeated look of someone who had nothing to look forward to. The look that marks the beginning of a downward spiral there is no coming back from. Nick could almost see the light of the human spirit beginning to fade away.

Still, she might have been beautiful once.

With a sigh as deep as a timeless sleep, the woman patted Lenny's hand, glanced over at Nick, who awkwardly turned away, struggled to her feet, and walked slowly toward the door. Lenny jumped up from his chair and followed her into the night.

"She needs a blanket," Daniel said, his eyes following the woman out the door.

"A blanket?" Nick asked.

"I saw a man lying on the floor using his shoes for a pillow. He had no blanket. I saw another man lay his own blanket over the man on the floor. I called it a blanket of kindness from a man who had nothing but shared everything. The Pear Lady needs a blanket of kindness."

Nick didn't know what to say. He just nodded his head and welcomed a friendly silence between the two of them while Daniel finished his meal. Minutes later the kid pushed his empty plate away. "Man, that was a good meal! Not as good as my Moms would have made but still good."

Citizen Daniel looked around the room, almost as though he was seeing it for the first time.

"You know why they call it a soup kitchen?" he asked Nick. Without waiting for

Nick to say anything, he answered his own question. "Because back during the Great Depression they opened places where people down on their luck could get a meal but the meal was always just vegetable soup and bread so they called them soup kitchens."

Nick's thoughts went to Mae Rose. If she'd been around back then, he thought to himself, smiling, she would have had the best soup kitchen in town.

Daniel wasn't finished. "That gangster, Al Capone, actually started the first soup kitchen because he wanted people to think he was a good guy."

"You know what they say," Nick offered. "Everyone has *some* good in them."

Daniel's face darkened, like an evil shadow.

"No," he muttered. "Not everyone."

CHAPTER THIRTY-ONE

THE PEAR LADY

LENNY WALKED WITH THE PEAR LADY TO THE WOMEN'S SHELTER. HE put his hand on her shoulder.

"The days go by," he said. " Steady. Like box cars on a passing freight train. Some good, some not so good. Can't stop 'em. Best you can do is keep on believin' what you believe in. You'll get through."

"I know, Lenny." She gave him a weak smile. "I'm just going through a storm right now. I'll get over it. Thanks for listening to my sob story."

"No problem."

It began to snow. Tiny flakes, dancing their way down an invisible staircase connecting heaven to earth, pausing to blow a kiss to Lenny and the Pear Lady on their way by.

"I think I'm just going to stand out here for awhile, Lenny. You should get going."

"You gonna be okay? I could stay."

"I'm fine. Really. Go get warm somewhere. I'll see you around."

Lenny nodded, turned and walked away. Stopped, turned back and pointed a finger at the Pear Lady.

"Better days," he said. "Better days ahead."

~

I HAVE ALWAYS THOUGHT *of Christmas as a good time;*

The Pear Lady stood in the falling snow, reliving the memory of her mother enchanting her with the magic of Charles Dickens on Christmas Eves so long ago.

... a kind, forgiving, generous, pleasant time; a time when men and women seem to open their hearts freely, and so I say, God bless Christmas!

Her mother loved Christmas.

"Christmas is a whole heart full of feelings," she would tell her young daughter.

"What kinds of feelings, Mama?"

"The kind I get when I hug you, heart to heart."

And she would wrap her arms around the girl who would one day become the Pear Lady and squeeze all the love from her own heart into her daughter's heart.

So long ago.

The Pear Lady was sixty-three years old now.

Alone.

And homeless.

And hurting because today, less than three weeks before Christmas, *a time when men and women seem to open their hearts freely,* she had been robbed.

An extra pair of shoes, two extra pairs of socks, a can opener, a bag of coins, a sandwich, three used teabags, a bottle of water, a purse and five Christmas pears, all stuffed into a duffel bag she'd found at the mission.

Gone.

The snow turned cold. The night turned cold. The Pear Lady felt it in her feet first. Some days the winter cold was so cruel her socks froze to the bottom of her feet and she couldn't be certain when she undressed for the night if she was peeling off her socks or her skin.

She shivered. Went into the shelter.

The other women in the shelter, thirty-one of them on this night, stole a look at her, avoided her eyes. They knew her pain, her loss. They'd all been there.

No one said anything.

The Pear Lady, sixty-three and homeless, stood under the hot water in the shower longer than the allotted fifteen minutes.

No one said anything.

When she finally made her way back to bottom bunk #17, she found a torn and tattered valise next to her pillow, a makeshift Christmas bow attached to its handle. Inside were four pair of socks, two pair of shoes, a sandwich bag filled with loose change, a woolen shawl and a box of teabags.

Looking up she saw thirty-one homeless women squeezing into the space between the bunks. As one, they opened their arms and gathered the Pear Lady into a blanket of kindness. It warmed her like a summer breeze, wrapped itself around her like her mother's arms and carried her to a place of tranquility that seemed almost holy.

The next morning, less than a few weeks before Christmas, thirty-two women, homeless but not alone, drifted arm-in-arm from the shelter into the uncertainty of another day on the street. Behind them, Scotch-taped to the door leading to the bunk room, a handwritten note:

When I had lost all my things, just when I lost all hope, you nested a pillow of faith beneath me and restored my feeling of belonging. TPL

CHAPTER THIRTY-TWO

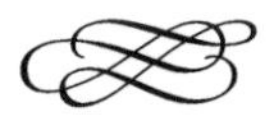

DANNI

The Pennsylvania sky was as clear blue as a mountain lake, the air as crisp as a new apple and the sun was just warming up to the idea of a shorter work day.

Danni Worthy stood on her tip toes and peered over the top of the snowdrifts that filled her sidewalk like a layer of overweight clouds fallen from grace. The wind had sculpted one section of the drifts into what looked like an ocean wave about to break onshore. Pretty, she had to admit. Prettier if it hadn't landed in the middle of her sidewalk.

"Good morning."

She stood a little taller on her toes, smiled brightly when she saw who the voice belonged to.

"You're back!"

"I'm out of cookies." Nick answered.

She laughed. "Me, too, but we've got a ton of hot chocolate."

Nick clapped his hands together. "Can't turn that down. If you'll throw me your shovel, I'll get to work."

Danni laughed again and tossed the shovel to the old saint. "Thank you, Santa, you're a life saver. Again."

"You don't have to call me Santa anymore. You can call me Nick."

She kept her eyes locked on him for several seconds, moving her gloved hands up and down, up and down, like she was juggling, or weighing melons. "Nick, Santa, Nick, Santa, Nick ... no ...you're Santa. It fits you. Don't ask me why 'cause I don't know, but it fits you." She turned toward the house. "Oh ..." She stopped, turned to face Nick and added, hand cupped over her mouth, "... keep your head down. I saw Roger out here a few minutes ago. He had a shovel in his hands, but if he sees you with a shovel in *your* hands ..." She lifted both of her arms into the air. "Just sayin'."

~

It took half an hour to clear the sidewalk. Danni was waiting on the front porch, a reindeer mug of steaming hot chocolate in her hands.

"As promised," she said, handing the mug to Nick. "Hope you don't mind the reindeer. I think it's Cupid 'cause see? it has a heart-shaped nose."

Nick shrugged and took a sip.

"Delicious!"

She waited till he'd taken a few more sips and then said, "I'm sorry for acting like a wuss."

"A wuss?"

"Yeah, you know, a jellyfish, a wimp, a girlie girl, you know."

"Why would I think that?"

She pointed to the sidewalk. "It's just snow. It falls, it clogs your sidewalk, you get out and shovel it. No big deal but ..." She looked at him, her brown eyes filled with need, took a deep breath of the wintery air around them, exhaled slowly and whispered, "I'm sorry. I need to say this to someone and ..." she tapped his shoulder, " ... tag, you're it."

She cleared her throat. "When I was a kid and it got to be Christmas time, my mother would take me to see Santa. I would sit on his lap and pull out my list of everything I thought was wrong with the world and I would say to Santa, 'Here's what I want for Christmas, Santa. I want you to make all of the sad and bad things in the world go away.' And he would give me this goofy smile and tell me to look at the camera and someone dressed like an elf would take our picture and that was that."

She took in another deep breath, puffed her cheeks and let it out.

"And here you are again, Santa, and I have a list that I can't talk to anyone else about because I'm supposed to be the strong one, the tough old bird. But I'm tired of being strong, so brace yourself Santa, because here it is. I lost my youngest daughter, Butterfly, less than a month ago. My only other daughter, Donna, is disappearing before my eyes. My husband is sick and nobody knows what's wrong with him. We're running out of money and .." she pointed at the sidewalk. "I can't even shovel snow anymore."

She didn't cry. She didn't pout. She just nodded her head sharply and said, "Whoo! That felt good! Thank you, Santa. Back to work."

And she was gone.

Nick stood on the porch staring at the reindeer mug for more than a minute before saying, "You don't look anything like Cupid."

He left the mug on the porch, picked up the shovel and began clearing snow from the driveway.

~

TWO HOURS LATER.

"You did a nice job, Santa."

Danni Worthy and Nick sat on her front porch, staring straight ahead, sipping more hot chocolate.

"I'm not Santa, I'm just Nick."

"Does Roger know you shoveled him out, too?"

"I don't think so. The last time I saw him , about an hour ago, he threw his shovel in the air and went inside."

She turned to look at him, appraising him, like he was an unexpected treasure brought home from a yard sale. "Who are you, Santa, Nick, and where did you come from?"

He smiled, let out a little grunt. "You wouldn't believe me if I told you." A pause, a sideways glance. "How are you feeling?"

"I'm good. And I apologize for my pity party. I don't know what happened. You were there and it all just ..." She flipped her hand into the air. "... fell out of my mouth. Those things I said, they 're not the kinds of things you ask Santa Claus to fix, they're the kinds of things you ask God to fix. You know, life, death, sickness. That's His thing, not Santa's."

I'll take care of it.

"But you wrote it all down for Santa. Why didn't you write it all down for God?"

She raised her mug of hot chocolate skyward. "I don't have His address."

CHAPTER THIRTY-THREE

THE SKIPPER

THEY SAT AWHILE LONGER, BOTH OF THEM THINKING THEIR THOUGHTS, neither of them sharing, enjoying the sun on their faces before Danni thanked Nick one more time and went inside to the realities awaiting her. Nick walked across the street to the little cottage-style house and shoveled the snow from Mae Rose's sidewalk. After returning the shovel to Danni's front porch, he made his way down the street to the park, swept the snow from the bench, sat, and waited, hoping to see little Donna Worthy on her way home from school.

DONNA SAW him before he saw her. He was a stranger, dressed kinda weird and, even weirder, he knew her name. But he was nice. And he knew about butterflies. Her mother told her almost every day that if she wasn't certain about something or someone in her way, go around it. "Take the long way, not the wrong way."

She walked into the park.

DONNA WORTHY LAY in the snow, making a Butterfly angel, swishing her arms and legs up and down, in and out, up and down, in and out.

"How was school today?" Nick called, not getting up off the bench.

She didn't look at him, spoke instead to the air above her. "It's different now. Mostly, I want to be alone. Sometimes the other kids laugh at me. It makes me mad."

"When you feel like that, you can make yourself disappear, like a Skipper."

"What's a Skipper?"

"It's a butterfly. Some people call it the disappearing butterfly because you can be looking right at it and blink and it's gone. When it's flying, it looks like its turning somersaults, like a falling leaf trying to keep its balance. It moves so quickly that even when you think you might see one, there could be dozens of them, all disappearing before your very eyes. So, you see, if you were a Skipper, you could disappear from what was making you angry and, by the time anyone saw you again, you wouldn't be angry anymore."

Still looking up to heaven, Donna asked, "How do I get to be a Skipper?"

"Close your eyes," Nick answered. "And pretend."

She closed her eyes. Couldn't see anything or anyone and pretended then, that nothing and no one could see her. It didn't take long before she imagined herself disappearing and the longer she kept her eyes closed, the deeper she disappeared, into a place where a sister could wear a dress and not be afraid that it would tear her skin; where a sister could let her hair hang in her face and not have to worry about swelling and blistering; where a sister could hug a sister and feel only joy; a place she wished she could be forever, with a sister, *her* sister, Butterfly. Donna Worthy was a Skipper and it felt ... freeing.

Like a butterfly escaping from a spider's web.

She lay there, not daring to open her eyes, not daring to move, not wanting the feeling to ever go away. When she did finally open her eyes and look over at the bench, the old man was gone. Disappeared.

Like a Skipper.

Nick watched from behind a tree; watched Donna Worthy lay, eyes closed, in the snow, disappearing into her imagination; watched her smile; watched her scrunch her eyes tightly shut, like someone not wanting to wake from a dream sent down from the stars; watched her finally stand, look around, shrug and wander, with her head up, from the park.

It was time.

Tomorrow, when he saw Donna Worthy, he would tell her the truth.

Bedtime in the sweet-smelling house. Donna Worthy did not reach under her bed, did not pull out her sketch pad, did not draw any pictures of a girl with butterfly wings. Instead, she pulled her warm winter comforter up to her chin and pretended. Pretended that Butterfly could be a Skipper angel if she wanted to and Donna was certain she would want to; pretended that Skipper Butterfly angel was in the room with her, fluttering, somersaulting invisibly, all around.

"Did Butterfly just flutter by?" she whispered and was almost positive she heard Butterfly squeal.

CHAPTER THIRTY-FOUR

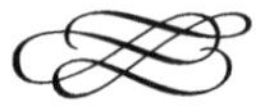

VOICES

NICK LAY ON A BOTTOM BUNK AT ST. PATRICK'S HAVEN LISTENING TO the voices in his head.

DANNI WORTHY: *Those things I said, they 're not the kinds of things you ask Santa Claus to fix, they're the kinds of things you ask God to fix. You know, life, death, sickness. That's His thing, not Santa's.*

NICK: I *did* ask God.

GOD: *I'll take care of it.*

THEY'D BEEN NAGGING at him, relentlessly, like an unsolved problem, since Lights Out two hours ago. Tossing his blanket aside, he flung his legs over the edge of the bed and sat, head in hands, thumbs massaging his temples.

. . .

WHERE WAS Grodan when you needed insight?

CHAPTER THIRTY-FIVE

THE NORTH POLE

TWENTY-FOUR DEGREES BELOW ZERO.

Not a night to be outside.

Grodan, the elder elf, *was* outside, in his slippers, in his pajamas, wrapped in his qiviut comforter. Qiviut, the inner wool of the muskox and, they say, the warmest wool in the world.

Watching the Northern Lights ebb and flow through the sky, like a ghostly waltz being played out on a phantom dance floor. There were those who believed the phenomenon truly was the dance of the ghost but Grodan knew it was no more than what it was - an act of God, designed to entertain, inspire and remind all of humankind that they are, after all, only human.

The moon was full and bright, biding its time while the aurora did its dance. It might last a few minutes, it might last a few hours but eventually it would tire and then quietly retire. The music of the night would resume and the moon, as always, would have the last dance.

Mrs. called from the porch of the big house. "Have you found him?"

"Yes," the elder elf called back, nodding his head and waving his arm in a somewhere-out-there direction. "He's in Erie, Pennsylvania."

"My goodness! What could be going on in Erie, Pennsylvania?"
"More than he thinks."

CHAPTER THIRTY-SIX

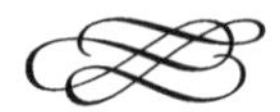

ST. PATRICK'S HAVEN

THE OTHER FIVE MEN IN THE ROOM DID NOT KNOW THAT NICK WAS awake, violently shaking his head from side to side trying to pry himself free of the echoes of his mind. Nor would they care. "Let us sleep," they would say. Morning would come soon enough and all too soon after that they would be back on the streets, dealing with the hunger, the exhaustion, the hopelessness, the life of the invisible.

UNTIL THEN, they were in a place where it was safe to close their eyes, a place where a hot shower had washed away the stress and the dirt and the smell of the life they led, cleansing them both physically and emotionally, if even for just one night.

NICK MOVED SILENTLY from the room.

~

01:12 a.m.

. . .

Nick stood on the warm side of the window looking up at a million stars poking holes in the canopy of darkness above him. He had seen and been in some of the world's most immense and humbling skies, submerged in an ocean of stars drifting through a universe that, like time, had no beginning, no middle, no end.

He remembered counting stars in the endless sky over the Atacama Desert in Chile, the Namib Desert in South Africa, the skies over New Zealand and Hawaii and Canada. He knew that many of the stars he'd counted were wishing stars, but he never knew which ones. No one did. Grodan once told him, "When you look to the sky with a wish on your heart, a wish that is honorable, sincere and God-given, the wishing star will come to you."

"I could use a wishing star right now," Nick whispered into the night.

By coincidence, or divine intervention, one of the best places in the world for star gazers was just one hundred and fifty miles from St. Patrick's Haven - a place called Cherry Springs State Park where the heavens regularly put on a light show. Aquarius, Aquila, the Eagle, Orion, the Hunter, Ursa Major, the Great Bear and dozens more constellations; the Milky Way, the Northern Lights, meteor showers, a never-ending tapestry suspended in the night sky like a mobile over the cradle of Baby Earth. So, why not a wishing star?

"Why not?" Nick whispered again.

He felt something stir inside him. Hope? Then something else. Guilt. There were children out there, all over the world, staring up at this very same sky, hoping and wishing with all their heart. Who was he, the man who used to be Santa Claus, to dare to ask for one of their wishing stars?

He puffed out his cheeks, held a second, let the air fizzle out of his mouth and then sagged against the wall. Like a flat tire.

"Yer lookin' a little low there, buddy."

"Who?" Nick squinted into the darkness, trying to focus on where the voice had come from. A disembodied voice in the night. Like a Bogeyman.

A shadowy figure holding a walking stick limped toward him. "It's just me, Nick."

"Lenny? I didn't know you were here tonight."

Lenny shrugged. "What about you? Aren't you supposed to be long gone outta town by now?"

"Things got a little complicated, but by this time tomorrow I should be gone."

"You gonna do your Invisible Man trick again?"

. . .

"I wish."

"Careful what you wish for there, Nicky boy."

CHAPTER THIRTY-SEVEN

THE OTHER MAN

DANNI LOOKED AT HER SMILING DAUGHTER AND SAW A LIGHT IN HER eyes she hadn't seen since before Butterfly died. She was reminded of The Miracle at Quecreek Mine when, after being trapped underground for seventy-seven hours, nine Pennsylvania miners looked up and saw a light and knew, "We're gonna be okay."

Donna Worthy looked up from her sketch pad. "What did you say, Mom?"

Danni hadn't realized she'd been thinking out loud.

"Oh, nothing. Just talking to myself. What are you drawing?"

"Skippers," She held up the tablet. "See?"

"But, I don't see anything?"

"That's cause they're the invisible butterflies. No one can see them."

"Oh, I see. Wait, I guess I don't see." she said with a sly smile. "Is that one of your Dad's butterfly stories?"

"No, the other man told me about the Skippers."

"The other man?"

"Uh-huh. The man in the park."

Danni Worthy felt like the wind had just been kicked out of her. Careful not to alarm her daughter, she asked, in a voice as steady as she could manage, "What man in the park, sweetheart?"

"The man in the Santa Claus suit."

CHAPTER THIRTY-EIGHT

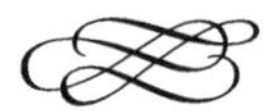

THE ARREST

THE AVERAGE DAILY TEMPERATURE IN ERIE, PENNSYLVANIA IN December is thirty-six degrees. When Nick arrived at the park a little past noon, the temperature was fifty-eight degrees and climbing. It was as if the warming wind the Chinook Indians called the Snow Eater had lost its sense of direction and leap-frogged the Rocky Mountains, Montana and Wyoming, its usual haunts, and blown due east on a collision course with the city by the lake, like a random act of nature on a whirlwind tour.

Whatever had caused the warming trend didn't matter much to Nick as he settled onto the bench in the park, closed his eyes, locked both hands behind his head, leaned back and let the warm breeze slow dance across his face. He could hear a dray of squirrels chattering optimistically in the trees; he could hear the snow melting, dripping in rhythm from the branches, like someone had left a tap running and, in the distance, a crow, warning everyone that this anomaly was just a cruel joke and the last laugh would be on all of them. Nick couldn't help but smile. It was one of those days when it felt good to be alive.

"Excuse me, sir?"

Nick opened his eyes. Flanking him were two police officers, one man, one woman, both with one hand on their weapon.

Nick looked up at the two officers, his face full of questions.

The woman spoke first.

"Would you please stand up, sir? We need you to come with us."

"You want me to go with you?"

"Yes, sir," the woman answered. "Please stand up." She was tall, at least five foot nine, trim, athletic, blond hair cut short, wide blue eyes. The fingers of her free hand drummed back and forth across the handcuffs on her belt. Her partner, easily six-foot two, looked like molten lead poured into a uniform. He was clean shaven, had a Roman nose, tight set jaw and riveting brown eyes riveted, at the moment, on Nick.

Nick stood. "Where are we going?"

"To the station, sir," the man answered.

"The station?" Nick asked.

"The police station, sir."

Nick pushed both hands in front of him, like a mime pushing up against a wall only he could see.

"If this is about me being Santa Claus for you and your fellow officers, I'm afraid you've got the wrong man."

"I think we have the right man, sir," the male officer said, reaching for Nick. "Let's go."

Without another word, both officers gripped Nick's arms, one on each side of him and, like a pair of ushers, escorted him to their cruiser. As he was being lowered into the back seat, Nick turned and saw Danni Worthy watching from the other side of the park. He smiled and gave her a wave.

She did not wave back.

DANNI WORTHY WATCHED from the edge of the park as the police officers escorted Nick to their cruiser. She had trusted him, believed him, opened up to him.

"I thought there was good in you. I felt it."

What she felt now was betrayed, deceived, verbally seduced by a smooth-talking old man whose way to Danni's daughter was through her mother.

"Judas!"

Just as she spat the word, Nick turned, saw her standing there and gave her a weak smile followed by a wave.

The temperature may have hit fifty-eight degrees but Danni felt a shiver run through her, like Death itself had just traced its cold, bony finger down her spine.

DONNA WORTHY COULDN'T WAIT to get to the park, couldn't wait to see the man who dressed like Santa Claus, couldn't wait to tell him what a good day it had been at school, mostly because he had taught her how to be a Skipper and she had been able to disappear three times! She ran from the school bus stop to the park, her backpack thumping along behind her.

He wasn't there.

But he was always there. At least it seemed like it. So she sat on the bench and waited.

And waited.

And waited until she knew that if she didn't go home soon, her mother would come looking for her. With a heavy sigh, she rose off the bench, went and lay on her back in the melting snow and made a Butterfly angel.

Minutes later, she trudged home. Stomped home, maybe.

Not such a good day after all.

THE WEATHER finally came to its senses just after dark and, by nine that night, the temperature had dropped thirty-one degrees.

Mae Rose, bundled inside a heavy flannel pajama top that Franklin, God rest his soul, had no further need for, pulled the down comforter that she had made herself and snuggled under with

Franklin for all those years, up to her nose, rolled onto her side to let the bony gray cat curl into the small of her back, closed her eyes and dreamed of better days. Soup days.

In the house across the street, Danni Worthy lay in Donna's bed, holding her daughter close to her heart, breathing in as the child breathed out, absorbing every breath into her senses. She would stay there through the night.

A few blocks down the street, not far from an empty park bench, visible only by the light of the moon, an angel lay frozen to the ground. A Butterfly angel.

CHAPTER THIRTY-NINE

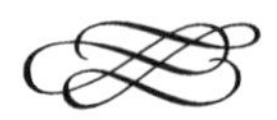

A BUTTERFLY IN HEAVEN

AMBER WORTHY WAS ONE IN A MILLION.

Perfect.

Perfect soft as maple syrup doe-brown eyes, perfect smile that lit up her face and any other face in the room and perfect celestial, upturned nose that, according to legend, was a nose given only to eternal optimists.

Perfect.

Except for the tiny blister on her heel that quickly became two, then three, then too many to count.

"Your daughter is a Butterfly Child," the doctor told them. "And I'm sorry but that isn't as pleasant as it sounds."

Amber Worthy. One in a million.

The one in a million born with Junctional epidermolysis bullosa - skin as fragile as a butterfly wing - and the rarest and most severe form of the disease.

She never complained.

Not when her skin would blister and burst into open, burning wounds; not when her bath water could be no warmer than body temperature; not when her food could never be warmer than lukewarm and had to be fed to her through a syringe or an eyedropper; not even when her voice became only a weak, rasping sound.

Like a butterfly crying for help.

She never complained.

Not when her diapers needed extra padding at the legs and waist; not when all her clothing needed to be as loose-fitting as possible, hanging from her body like Spanish moss over a myrtle tree and worn inside-out with tags, cuffs and necklines removed; not even when she had to wear slippers and socks so thick and padded she could hardly walk without tipping over.

They called her Butterfly.

She would wait, hidden behind the door, for her father to come home and then flit past him in her wobbly shoes. He would laugh and ask, *"Did a butterfly just flutter by?"* Butterfly would squeal with delight and her father's heart would both soar and shatter.

Whenever her sister, Donna, took her for a ride in her wagon, tucked safely inside a fortress of pillows, Butterfly begged her, *"Go faster, Donna! Go faster!"* so that the breeze on her face would feel like a thousand butterfly kisses happening all at once. She couldn't ask for a real butterfly kiss because if someone flicked their eyelashes against her skin it would tear and burn.

"Kisses aren't supposed to hurt, Mama."

"One day it won't hurt anymore, my love. Nothing will hurt anymore."

And Danni would sing her daughter to sleep, *"I'll be a butterfly tucked in your hair, to softly kiss you and whisper I care."*

And Butterfly, wrapped in her ultra-soft sheepskin pajamas, snuggling deep into her water mattress, would answer back ...

"Blow puffs on my face, Mama."

When Butterfly was old enough, her dad took her and Donna to the park every Saturday, where he told them butterfly stories too impossible to believe.

Butterfly's favorite was the story of the Amber Phantom butterfly.

"It has wings you can see right through," her father told her.

Butterfly fell asleep that night imagining her skin was made of wings she could see right through. Skin that didn't hurt.

The day after Thanksgiving, six months before her fifth birthday, Butterfly was rushed to the hospital with a fever, chills, rapid heart beat and shortness of breath. An infection called sepsis had worked its way into her bloodstream and spread, unstoppable, throughout her body. Her mother was there. Her father was there. Her sister was there. They looked scared.

"It's okay," she whispered in that raspy voice. "I'm going into my cocoon now."

She closed her eyes.

Opened them in heaven.

With a butterfly perched on her nose.

She giggled, reached for it but it quickly tip-toed up her nose, fluttered its wings against her face and flew off into a blanket of purple flowers. Her very first real butterfly kiss.

And it didn't hurt.

She laughed out loud. Someone laughed back. Then someone else. Then someone else. Laughter. Children's laughter. Butterfly stepped gingerly toward the sound.

It didn't hurt.

Another step.

It didn't hurt.

She laughed out loud. Someone laughed back.

Butterfly ran toward the laughter.

It didn't hurt.

Nothing hurt anymore.

CHAPTER FORTY

POP

NICK SAT STARING ACROSS THE DESK AT A MAN WITH SKIN THE COLOR OF burnt bronze and whose name tag said he was Detective A. Popporicht. He looked just this side of middle-age with a full head of hair overdue for a trim and quiet gray eyes set deep into a kindly, almost grandfatherly face, overdue for a shave.

"Pop" was legendary, not famous. Famous were the Special Victims cops on TV. Legendary was the real cop, the man called Pop, who made it his business to put predators out of business. Consensus around the department was that it had something to do with Pop's own childhood, but no one ever asked and Pop never offered. Whatever the reason, protecting children was Pop's life work.

Also legendary were Pop's visits to elementary schools throughout the state, lecturing children and parents on the dangers of child predators. Danni Worthy had been to one of Pop's lectures, *Take the Long Way, Not the Wrong Way*. She had never forgotten it and, in turn, never let her girls forget it.

"So, Nick," the legend began, his voice as deep as a water barrel. "Nick who?"

"Just Nick."

Pop huffed his disapproval. "I'll tell you what, Just Nick. My name is Popporicht. Detective Abraham Popporicht. My friends call me Pop. You are not my friend, so you can call me Detective or Detective Popporicht or even Mr. Popporicht. See what I'm trying to get to here?"

"No."

Pop leaned back in his chair, squinted his eyes almost shut, pursed his lips.

"What I'm trying to get to, Just Nick, is that I'm introducing myself, *all* of myself, to you, expecting you to introduce all of *yourself* right back to me."

"There is no more, Detective. It's just Nick. Can you tell me why I'm here?"

"We'll get to that ... Just Nick ... but first ..." He pushed his chair away from the desk, stood and gathered some papers. "I'm going to have someone come take your fingerprints. I've got a machine back there," he thumbed over his shoulder, "that has more than a hundred and seventy-four million fingerprints stored inside. You sit tight, Just Nick. I'll be back in a few minutes and chances are pretty good that I'll be able to tell you who you really are."

As the detective lumbered his way through a row of desks and disappeared around a corner, Nick took in his surroundings. He'd never been inside a police station. What had at first glance appeared to be a row of desks looked now more like a steel jungle of desks littered with files, photos and sticky notes scattered haphazardly throughout the room, like shopping carts in a Walmart parking lot. Common to every desk were a computer, a landline phone and a roll-away chair. One desk stood out. The one with the miniature Christmas tree next to a handmade sign reading, *Secret Santa Gifts Here.*

Nick waited.

Someone took his fingerprints.

And waited.

Someone else took his picture with their phone.

And waited.

Phones rang, detectives came and went, minutes turned to hours, lights dimmed. The mood in the room softened from high anxiety to tomorrow's another day.

Nick dozed.

"You like kids, Just Nick?"

Nick jerked out of his nap like he'd been slapped. Detective Abraham Popporicht was back behind the desk, staring hard at Nick.

"I love kids." Nick answered.

"Little girls?"

"Girls, boys. I love all the children."

The detective shuddered visibly, sat straight up in his chair and leaned in as close to Nick as the desk that separated them would allow.

"How about Donna Worthy, Just Nick? Do you love her?"

"Donna? How do you know ...?"

"What makes Donna Worthy worth so much attention, Nick?"

Nick leaned back in his chair, twisting away from the detective's prying eyes as the reality of what was happening finally dawned on him.

"Are you trying to say that I would hurt Donna Worthy?"

"I'm not trying to say anything. How about you say something?"

"How about if I show you something, Detective?"

Nick dug into his pocket, pulled out two crumpled pieces of paper and handed them to the detective.

"What's this?"

"Letters."

Detective Popporicht eyed Nick suspiciously before lowering his eyes and reading the two letters, looking up at Nick every few seconds.

"Where'd you get these, Just Nick?"

"They were sent to me."

"They were sent to Santa Claus. Are you trying to tell me you're Santa Claus?"

"I *was* Santa Claus, Detective." He hesitated. "Now I'm not."

"Listen, mister, I don't know where you got these letters," Pop said, waving the letters in Nick's face. "And I don't know what kind of game you're playing, telling me you're Santa Claus ..."

"*Was* Santa Claus."

"Whatever, but I do know that I have ..." He tap-tap-tapped a piece of paper on the desk. "... a Restraining Order ordering you to stay away from Donna Worthy, her mother, her father, her house and the park where she plays!" He took a breath. "And you know what else I know, Just Nick? Nothing! I know nothing else! According to the more than one hundred and seventy-four million fingerprints on file, you don't exist, Just Nick!"

"A lot of people think I don't exist," Nick said softly, looking the detective in the eyes. "And after tomorrow, it'll be true."

Nick rose out of the chair. "I'm leaving now."

He wound his way through the steel jungle of desks. Detective Popporicht called after him, "If you go near Donna Worthy or her family, I'll be coming for you, Just Nick. Count on it!"

He looked again at the letters Nick had given him.

DEAR SANTA CLAUS,

MOM SAYS YOU MIGHT NOT COME TO OUR HOUSE THIS YEAR BUT MY SISTER IS SICK SO WILL YOU PLEASE MAKE HER BETTER FROM THE NORTH POLE? THANK YOU, SANTA.

YOUR FRIEND,
DONNA WORTHY

DEAR SANTA CLAUS,

MY SISTER DIED. I THOUGHT YOU WERE GOING TO MAKE HER BETTER.

YOUR FRIEND,
DONNA WORTHY

CHAPTER FORTY-ONE

THE ATTACK

NICK WAS HUNGRY.

He could have been, should have been angry, frustrated, surprised, hurt, disappointed, confused and maybe he would be all of that later but at that moment, standing in front of the police station, he was hungry.

He looked around.

Minutes away was St Patrick's Haven, but too late now to secure a bed for the night and maybe a banana or an apple from Betsy. Also minutes away was the soup kitchen, but too late now to get a hot meal.

There was a Tim Hortons, open twenty-four hours, so close he could almost see it. Lenny had told him, "A guy mindin' his own business with a cuppa coffee over at the Tim Hortons is almost invisible. Should be no problem for the Invisible Man."

Nick checked his pockets. Twenty-two dollars and some change, still left from the forty dollars Roger had given him. More than enough for a cup of coffee.

He started walking.

~

THE MAN SITTING ALONE at the window table inside Tim Hortons closed his eyes, dipped the tip of his nose into his coffee cup and breathed in like he was breathing in a summer morning.

"Ahhhh, nothing like the smell of Tim Hortons coffee!" he almost giggled to himself.

The kid behind the counter ignored him. He seemed harmless.

"No, not smell, silly ... aroma? Yes, that's it! Nothing like the *aroma* of Tim Hortons coffee!"

He took a sip, smiled opened his eyes and let his gaze wander to the street outside.

"No way!"

He shook his head, hard, looked again, pushing his face tight against the window.

"No way!" He almost yelled it this time.

He had heard that the police had taken him away. He had heard why. So why was the guy who looked like Santa walking free, right there, right now?

The darkness crept toward him.

"No!" He tried to swat it away like a pesky fly but it kept coming. It always kept coming, like a distant ocean wave, moving closer and closer until it exploded over him and sent him swirling into an abyss as deep and as dark as the shadow of death.

The air around him went deathly cold, suddenly filled with a suffocating, paralyzing presence of evil. He couldn't breathe, couldn't speak, couldn't hear, couldn't feel. There was no face to this darkness, nothing physical - just a metaphysical presence of evil stealing through the room like a plague. Wrapping his arms tightly around himself, the man at the window table began to sway back and forth, begging the darkness to go away, go away, go away.

But the darkness stayed. It always stayed.

The man at the window table lurched to his feet and stumbled blindly through the coffee shop, knocking a Santa Claus bobblehead from the cash register on his way out.

~

NICK SMILED at the sight of a familiar face charging through the door, the scent of coffee suddenly filling the air. Maybe it wouldn't be such a long, lonely night after all.

"Nothing like the smell of coffee, don't you think?" Nick called to the man rushing toward him.

"Coffee doesn't smell, *Dad*! Coffee has an aroma!"

Dad?

"You talked your way out of it again, didn't you, Dad? Got them to let you go again? Free as bird. Not again, Dad. Never again."

Those were the last words Nick heard before the man knocked him to the ground and began pounding his head into the sidewalk.

THE KID behind the counter called 911. Three men, one with a cast on his arm, pulled the attacker off Nick and held him until the police came. A woman, the one known as the Pear Lady, wrapped her sweater around Nick's head and cradled it in her lap, looking skyward, eyes filling with tears and whispering, "Please, God, not again!" over and over until the paramedics arrived and rushed Nick to the hospital.

He died before they got him there.

CHAPTER FORTY-TWO

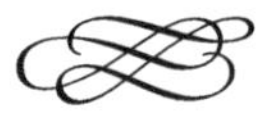

THE NORTH POLE

MRS. STAGGERED BACKWARD LIKE THE FLOOR HAD SUDDENLY TILTED beneath her. Steadying herself with one hand on the old oak table, she grabbed at her chest with the other, feeling like a piece of her heart had just been ripped away.

"SANTA!" she screamed and then ran from the big house, calling for Grodan.

GRODAN LOOKED SKYWARD. Ulama, the Devil Bird, winged past him so close he could feel the terror oozing from the wings of the Omen of Death.

"SANTA!" he yelled and then ran toward the big house, calling for Mrs..

CHAPTER FORTY-THREE

HEAVEN

HEAVEN CAN BE EVERYTHING YOU IMAGINE IT TO BE. UNTIL YOU GET there. Nick had been there more than once. But this time it felt different, was different. This time he was on a hilltop flooded with purple wildflowers unlike any he'd ever seen.

They were called Godsend.

Far below, a river with no beginning and no end wandered idly through a secluded valley, rays of light ricocheting from its surface like falling stars bouncing off a trampoline.

And there was quiet. Not silence. Quiet, like daybreak in the woods where you can feel life all around you but what you hear is the quiet.

"Hello?" Nick called, his voice echoing off into the endless plain of peace. "Can anyone hear me? Is anyone here?"

"I am."

"God?" Nick twirled full circle to find himself suddenly dwarfed beneath the tallest Scotch Pine he had ever seen. There were no decorations on the tree, only four Star of Bethlehem flowers, one each on branches facing north, south, east and west.

Purity, honesty, innocence and hope.

"A compass for anyone losing their way." Nick spoke so softly he wasn't sure he'd spoken aloud. Even more softly, he added, "That's me."

"Who are you?" God asked.

"I'm Nick."

A patient silence and then ...

"Who are you?" God asked again.

"I am ... *was*, Santa Claus."

"Who ... are ... you?" God's voice rumbled impatiently, expectantly.

"I am ... Santa Claus." With his head down, Nick mumbled, "That's who I am. Santa Claus. The failure."

A warmth and a calm washed over him, like the August waves washing over the shores of Lake Erie.

"You have not failed at being who you are," God spoke softly now. "You have failed at being who you are not."

"Is that why I died?"

"It is why you are here."

"I don't understand."

A fifth Star of Bethlehem floated to the ground beneath the giant Scotch Pine.

Forgiveness.

And God spoke. Of a journey

And God spoke again. "Go back."

"Back?"

"The child needs you."

"But I failed her. I failed You. How can I be of any use to anyone?"

God's voice came even softer, gentler, like a mother, a father, a grandmother, a grandfather, a friend. "See who you are. Be who you are."

As he was being tugged from heaven, away from the hilltop flooded with purple wildflowers, away from the river with no beginning and no end and away from the holy quiet, like a pebble being tugged back into the lake by the receding August waves of Lake Erie, Nick took a deep, deep breath of the air surrounding the giant Scotch Pine.

"Like a walk in the forest."

CHAPTER FORTY-FOUR

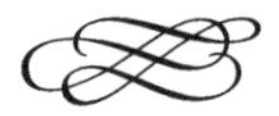

POP

NICK AWOKE IN A HOSPITAL BED.

His head hurt. His back hurt. His ribs hurt. His heart hurt.

"What happened?" Nick wondered aloud.

"That's what I want to know," a man's voice answered.

Nick squinted at the familiar face hovering over him.

"Detective?"

" Popporicht. Yeah, me again and you again, together again. How's your head, Just Nick?"

"It hurts."

"Well, from what they tell me, you took a pretty bad beating. Or a pretty *good* beating, depending on how you look at it. They said you even died on the way to the hospital and then out of the blue you just all of a sudden sat up ranting and raving about some kind of tree. They said it was like a miracle. Hey, it's Christmas. Why not? You'll be happy to know we got the guy that assaulted you."

"Someone assaulted me? I died?"

"Yeah and yeah. The guy's right here in this hospital in the Psych Ward. He says he gets blackouts, doesn't remember anything. How about you, Just Nick? What do *you* remember? Do you know the guy?

Does he know you? Did you mess with his kid? Did he know you were stalking Donna Worthy? Did you ..."

"STOP!" Nick swung his arms open wide, lifting the water jug and the box of tissues from the overbed table into the air and across the room.

"Oops, did I hit a nerve there, Just Nick?" An almost innocent smile, somewhat like a Mississippi politician might practice, snaked its way across the detective's face.

A nurse rushed into the room.

CHAPTER FORTY-FIVE

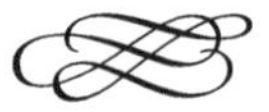

THE PSYCH WARD

THE MAN WHO ASSAULTED NICK PACED.

AND PACED.

AND PACED, like a caged cat, around a room smaller than a walk-in closet, grabbing at the locked door again and again, hoping again and again that it would somehow magically open. It never did and no matter how long and how loud and how often he called for someone, no matter how many times he pounded on that locked door, no one came.

HE SAT down onto a bed bolted to the floor, staring at blank, colorless walls and then lay back to stare at a colorless ceiling, seeing for the thousandth time and wondering for the thousandth time how someone had managed to scratch the word *help* into one of the ceiling tiles. His eyes grew heavy. He slept. The nightmare pounced.

. . .

He was a boy again, flying again, tied into a rope swing dangling between the first and third floor of the tumbledown apartment building. "Let's go flying, my love," Mommy would say, strapping him tightly into the rope swing and lowering it carefully out the window. The boy did not know that while he was flying, Daddy was chasing Mommy, throwing things, hitting and hurting; he did not know why, when the bad noises stopped and Daddy was gone, Mommy would pull him back inside and hug him so tightly his voice went squeaky; he did not know that she was saving his life. Then came the last time he flew - the time he heard Daddy's voice from above, "Well, well, well, what do we have here?" And Daddy lifted the flying boy back into the apartment and ...

"No!"

CHAPTER FORTY-SIX

SARGE

The nurse who had rushed into Nick's hospital room had just as quickly rushed Detective Popporicht out of the room, but not before the detective poked his thumb into his chest and said, *"They call me Pop, Just Nick, and Pop always gets the weasel."* He grinned, like a weasel, and was gone.

"I don't know who he thinks you are and I don't know who he thinks *he* is, coming in here and upsetting you like this," the nurse clucked, checking her patient's vitals, "but I'll tell the staff to keep him away from you." Satisfied that order had been restored, she patted his hand. "You get some rest now."

"Do you think I could walk for awhile?" Nick asked. "Walking calms me down."

"Hmmm, I know they want you walking so I don't see why not. Just go slowly. "

"Baby steps," Nick promised, inching slowly toward the door. "Point me in the right direction. I wouldn't want to accidentally wander onto the Psych Ward."

"Oh, we don't call it that anymore," she said, cupping her hand over her mouth. "It's called the Mental Health Unit and, not to worry about accidentally wandering into that horribly sad place, it's two floors up."

It was the first place Nick went.

AT THE END of fifty feet of corridor, cold and imposing, like armored sentries, stood two steel double doors with a phone on the wall next to them and the instruction, *Dial 0 for Assistance*. Nick dialed 0.

"What?" An impatient voice snapped.

"Hello. Can you let me in, please?"

"Who are you?"

"I'm Nick and I want to visit one of your patients."

A few seconds of silence. Then, "Is this a joke? Ted, is that you? Not funny, man."

"I'm not Ted, I'm Nick."

The double doors buzzed open with an urgency and out waddled a man, a short man, thick and round, like a bowl of pudding, stopping inches from Nick, standing on his tip toes and yelling, "How did you get out? No one gets out! Not on my watch!"

Nick took a few steps backwards.

"How could I get out if I haven't been in, Mister ..." said Nick, staring at the short man's name tag,"... Bagel?"

"*Bag*-el, like the bag. Not bagel like the donut! But you can call me Sarge!"

"Everything good out here, Bags?" echoed another man's voice from the corridor.

Both men turned to see a second security agent standing nervously between the double doors. He was tall but slim as a pencil. His eyes darted back and forth between Nick and Bagel like he was watching a tennis match.

"I told you never call me Bags," grumbled the little round man.

"Sorry ... Sarge."

"Better. And yeah, everything's good here. As a matter of fact, Ted ..." Smiling like a cobra, Sarge put his arm around Nick's shoulders and led him toward the double doors. "Nick here just dropped by for a visit."

"A visit?"

"Yeah. Why don't you take him and his merry old soul inside and introduce him around while I make some calls?"

The double doors whooshed shut behind the three of them, locking them into a small, sterile room with a hand-me-down steel desk sporting only a telephone, a box of Tums and a coffee mug emblazoned with the words, *My World, My Rules.* A few feet from the desk, on the far wall, were two more steel double doors.

Sarge pressed a button under the desk and the second set of steel double doors whooshed open onto a large room with several tables and chairs, most of them occupied by men and women, every one of them looking up expectantly as the doors opened. Ted nudged Nick into the room. The doors whooshed shut behind them.

TWO FLOORS down from the Mental Health Unit, Nurse Ellie Prather was losing patience with the man on the other end of the telephone.

"We don't call it the Psych Ward, Mr. Bagel, we call it the Mental Health Unit."

"Tomātoes, tomătoes, and it's Bag-el, like the bags, not bagel like the donuts! So, are you missing any looney tunes down there or not? 'Cause I got one up here with a cracked skull telling me he's just dropping by for a visit."

Nurse Prather glanced toward Nick's room. He was either in his room, asleep, or still out in the hallway, walking. Either way, he wasn't *missing.*

"All of my patients are accounted for, Mr. Bagel," she deliberately mispronounced his name. "Perhaps you should run a check on *your* patients? One of them may have slipped past you."

"It's Bag-el, like the bags and no one gets out of here! Not on my watch!"

The line went dead.

"EXCUSE ME."

Ted looked up from his crossword puzzle at Nick."

"Is everyone here?" Nick asked.

"Everyone?"

"All of the patients?"

"Oh. No, the patients out here are not a threat to themselves or anyone else. The others ..." Ted pointed his pen toward a bank of closed doors. "... we have to keep on lockdown. They're dangerous. Unpredictable."

"Thank you," Nick said with a smile. "I'll leave you to your puzzle. Sorry to have bothered you."

"No problem."

Nick bowed slightly toward Ted and went back to wandering, aimlessly it appeared, like the others in the room, looking like they had nowhere to go and wondering how they would get there. When he felt Ted's eyes no longer following him, Nick moved to the bank of doors, peering through the small window in each until he found the room he was looking for, the man he was looking for. The man in that room suddenly screamed, "No!" and leapt from the bed, both fists flailing into the empty air, tears pouring from his eyes.

With hope and a prayer, Nick touched his finger to his nose, imagined himself inside the room.

And went there.

Just in time to gather the panicked man into his arms, hold him close in a bear hug and rock him like a baby, not letting up or letting go until the trembling finally stopped. The man's breathing worked its way back to normal and the smell of fear left the room. Even then, the man collapsed deeper into Nick's arms, closed his eyes and let himself be held; let himself remember.

"My Moms used to hold me like this in the scary days."

Finally, he pulled away. Wiping his nose with the back of his hand, he opened his eyes.

Recognition.

"Citizen? Wow! What happened to you?"

DANIEL WAS on the edge of the bed talking to Nick who was standing against the wall out of sight of anyone who might look into the room.

""They took my phone," Daniel said, shaking his head, "... and my shoelaces and my belt and there 's always someone looking at me through that little window. It's kinda crazy. The food's okay. Not as good as my Moms used to make. Not even as good as what they give us at the soup kitchen, but it's okay. They don't have peanut butter. Isn't that weird? They don't have peanut butter. I don't like that they turn the lights out any time they want to. They told me I have to stay in this room because if they let me out I might hurt someone. The mean one, the one I'm supposed to call Sarge, said I already did hurt someone. I don't remember hurting anyone."

He looked at Nick.

"You never told me who hurt you, Citizen."

"It was someone who thought I was someone else."

"It's still not right. No one should hurt the senior citizens."

Nick nodded, said nothing. The redhead was only nineteen, maybe twenty years old, but right then, lying back onto the bed and curling up into as tight a ball as he could make himself, he looked like a lost, frightened boy.

"Can you get me out of here, Citizen? Please."

"I'm going to try."

BACK IN HIS OWN ROOM, two floors down, Nick was feeling more and more trapped. How could he get Daniel out of the Mental Health Unit and into a place where he would get the care he needed? What did he have to do to convince Detective Popporicht that he was not a predator? Most important, when and how would he be able to talk to Donna Worthy again? How?

How?

How?

Be who you are.

TWO FLOORS UP, Daniel sat on the edge of his bed and wondered how the senior citizen had gotten into his room and how was it possible that he had blinked and the old citizen was gone? Was it all a bad dream? Was he truly losing his mind? He lay back on the bed, stared up at the ceiling. *Help.*

CHAPTER FORTY-SEVEN

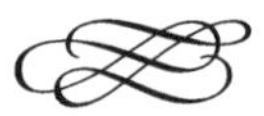

DONNA

DONNA WORTHY LAY ON HER BED STARING UP AT THE CEILING AT A poster of a butterfly. A Monarch, one of Butterfly's favorites. If she had wings, strong Monarch butterfly wings, Donna would fly all the way to heaven and find her sister and sneak her back home when God wasn't looking.

BUT DONNA WORTHY didn't have wings' and worse than that, it was getting harder and harder for her to be a Skipper, the disappearing butterfly. At first it was easy and it made her feel better, just like the Santa Claus man in the park said it would. But after awhile she started to feel like she was disappearing just so she could hide from the truth ... it was her fault that Butterfly had died. And every time she came back from disappearing, the emptiness was still there, the loneliness was still there, the sadness was still there. What wasn't there - was Butterfly.

SHE LOOKED up at the ceiling again.

. . .

WISHED SHE COULD FLY.

CHAPTER FORTY-EIGHT

DANNI

Dear God ... What next?

"That's it? That's all you got? *What next?*" Danni asked herself. Staring up at the kitchen ceiling like someone expecting all the right words to come tumbling down like manna from heaven, she was reminded of the handwritten sympathy card she and Joe had found in their mailbox shortly after Butterfly died. It said simply, *There are no words.* It was unsigned.

Butterfly had died, Donna had been stalked by an old man in a Santa suit, Joe was in the hospital with something called ALPINE Virus, money was getting so tight she was beginning to choke under the pressure, and all she could ask of God was W*hat next?*

Danni let out a subdued sigh and pushed herself away from the kitchen table, turning to put her cup of tea that had cooled, again, into the microwave, again. She pressed START. Nothing happened.

. . .

"WHAT NEXT?"

CHAPTER FORTY-NINE

BERN, SWITZERLAND

PROFESSOR MATHIAS PEDERSEN VOWED HE WOULD NOT REST UNTIL HE had solved the mystery of ALPINE Virus, a deadly strain of pneumonia that had infected dozens of people in Switzerland and put the rest of Central Europe on alert.

From his seat nearest the fireplace in the Einstein Cafe & bel étage in Bern's Old Town, the professor pushed his croissant aside and and checked his watch.

Two minutes.

Absentmindedly fingering the hook dangling from fishing line around his neck, he looked down at his notes. Pain, lung malfunction, infection, loss of awareness, loss of muscle function, loss of consciousness. The last word in the notes was circled in red with a question mark next to it. Fish?

One minute.

Maybe today was the day the clock would inspire him the way that same clock inspired Albert Einstein to create his Theory of Special Relativity years ago? The professor was not a superstitious man. What scientist is? He was a hopeful man. So - maybe today?

He picked up his pen. The clock struck. The crowd outside cheered. He waited.

Nothing.

Nothing new. Nothing different. Nothing else.

Not today.

Shuffling slowly out of the cafe, Professor Pedersen glanced up at the Clock Tower that was once a women's prison, housing women whose time had run out. These days, with every tick of the clock, the professor could not help but feel that time was also running out for thousands more.

Including a man in Erie, Pennsylvania.

A man named Joe Worthy.

CHAPTER FIFTY

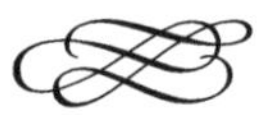

THE HOSPITAL

NICK STOOD IN HIS HOSPITAL ROOM, IN THE DARK, LOOKING OUT THE window, watching the snow fall in bunches, like it was being plowed carelessly from the clouds, not left on its own to drift aimlessly through the sky like something with nowhere particular to go and in no hurry to get there.

"It's time."

Nick turned in the direction of the voice, expecting to see a nurse or a doctor. There was no one there.

"Hello?" Nick called. "Is someone here?"

"I am."

"God?"

"It's time."

"Time for what?"

"To go home."

"Home? I can't go home. You told me there are things I have to do here."

"And you will."

"When?"

"You'll know."

"But ..."

Nick felt a warm hand cover his head. He felt his body quiver like a grove of aspen trees. His head no longer hurt. His back no longer hurt. Nothing hurt. He turned to look at his reflection in the window.

See who you are. Be who you are.

The door burst open. Sarge blew into the room, Nurse Prather tight on his heels..

"There he is! That's him! I told you! No one gets past me. Not on my watch!"

Nick turned to face Sarge and Nurse Prather.

"Oh," said Sarge, visibly disappointed.

"Oh!" said Nurse Prather, visibly confused.

In front of them stood a man fully dressed in a red suit. A man with a full white beard, thick white mustache, thicker white hair down to his shoulders and puffed out cheeks so rosy they seemed to glow in the dark.

A man called Santa Claus.

A man who touched his finger to his nose and disappeared.

CHAPTER FIFTY-ONE

ST. PATRICK'S HAVEN

St. Patrick's Haven is a sanctuary for twenty-four homeless men plus two full-time residents, both of whom have worked their way out of the odyssey of wandering the streets into "management" positions at the Haven. Their job is to keep the Haven, and its guests, in order, but their real talent lies in their ability to listen to men who need to vent to someone who understands, someone who's been there and not someone who sympathizes.

Santa was hoping to find one of the two managers still awake but it was already long past Lights Out and the only sounds he could hear were the sounds of the storm raging outside, sending everything in its path scattering like a thousand tin cans being kicked across a frozen lake.

The old saint moved silently into the kitchen where he found a notepad the size and shape of a milk jug pinned to a cork board next to the refrigerator. A ballpoint pen was clipped to the notepad. Santa unclipped the pen, tore two pages from the notepad and, by the gleam of a nightlight in the shape of a lighthouse, plugged into the wall by the stove, leaned over the counter and began to write. He wrote two notes, finishing the second just before a familiar voice sounded from the doorway.

"Lookin' for cookies, Nick?"

Santa turned to face the doorway. Lenny Schwartz squinted across the dimly lit kitchen at a man who looked just like the Santa Claus he'd seen in all the pictures.

"Oh, sorry, pal, I thought you was someone else," said Lenny, sounding a little disappointed, a little confused.

"I *was* someone else, but not anymore."

Santa put one of the notes on the counter, tapped it with his finger.

"Will you see to it that Betsy gets this note, please? And, Lenny, the next time you look in a mirror, see who you are and be who you are."

"What's that s'posed to mean?"

Santa put his finger to his nose and disappeared.

CHAPTER FIFTY-TWO

THE POLICE STATION

The Desk Sargent was not surprised to see a bearded man in a Santa Claus suit hurry into the police station. This week alone he had entertained the musings of a man dressed as a hot dog, another man dressed as a giant chicken and an elderly woman dressed in several layers of flowing chenille and holding a vial of pink water, claiming to be the Fountain of Youth. All part of the job. He *was* surprised that any of these characters would be out on a night like this.

"What can I do for you, Santa? Someone steal your sleigh?"

Santa handed the Desk Sargent a note. "Would you please see to it that Detective Popporicht gets this note?'

The Sargent took the note, wrote "For Pop" on it and leaned back to drop it into a memo tray.

. . .

LOOKING BACK TOWARD SANTA, the officer started to ask, "Who shall I say ...?"

THERE WAS NO ONE THERE.

CHAPTER FIFTY-THREE

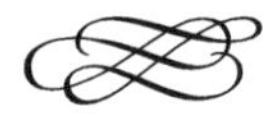

THE CAVE

DONNA WORTHY KEPT HER BEDROOM LIGHT ON. THE HOUSE FELT lonely. And empty. But at least with the light on, it didn't feel like she was in a cave. She was in a real cave once, with her dad. It was cold and drippy and there was a river in it but nobody knew where it came from. Creepy. People even got married in that cave. Creepier. She held her dad's hand the whole time they walked through that creepy cave. Her dad had big hands. They felt like stone on the top and sandpaper on the inside. They were like that, he told her, because of all the years he'd used them doing construction work. Before he got sick, he was working high in the sky in a crane, swinging a giant steel ball and knocking down buildings. Like Superman.

EXCEPT NOW HE was in the hospital. The last time Butterfly was in a hospital, she didn't come home. But Donna's dad would come home. He promised her he would and she believed him. Because he was Superman.

. . .

SHE COULD HEAR the snow tap, tap, tapping at her window like a ghost, trying to sneak inside. Her mom told her about a storm they had once on a Christmas Eve. There was so much snow it came right up to the bedroom windows. That might make it feel like she was inside a cave.

CREEPY.

~

SANTA STOOD outside Donna Worthy's house, the snow pounding down on him from above while, at the same time whirling up from the sidewalk at his feet. Like he was in a snow globe.

HE DIDN'T KNOW WHEN, he didn't know how, he didn't know why but he knew he would be back. Until then there was only one place to go. He touched his finger to his nose and went home.

CHAPTER FIFTY-FOUR

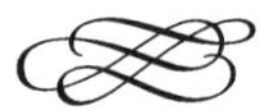

HOME

"MRS., I WAS A FOOL. I LOST SIGHT OF WHO I WAS AND LEFT YOU ALONE to do all that I should have been doing here while I went away and tried to do all that I should not have tried to do. And failed. Can you ever forgive me?"

Santa repeated the words over and over as he walked toward the big house, hoping, hoping, hoping. Long before he got there, Mrs. saw him and ran to him and threw her arms around him and kissed him.

Home.

THE NORTH POLE is near enough to heaven so that, on a clear night, you can hear the angels singing. This was one of those nights. Standing on one of the ice floes that wander aimlessly, like nomadic clouds across the Arctic Ocean, occasionally bumping into one another and then bouncing clumsily away like bumper cars at a carnival, Santa could hear the angels. Thousands upon thousands of voices flooding the heavens with joy and flowing through the old saint below like he was made of gauze.

As far from heaven as he was, Santa still believed he was standing on holy ground even though there was no ground beneath his feet. There was ice, anywhere from ten to sixty feet thick, and beneath that - water - the smallest ocean in the world but still about one and a half times the size of the United States.

Home.

Santa let his gaze wander through the darkness to the east. In a few months the sun would rise. It did that only once a year at the North Pole and it was not a sight to be squandered. Not a poet alive or dead would ever find the words to describe the longest of days nudging aside the longest of nights; when the moon bows its head to shield itself from the brilliance of another dawn; when the sky suddenly melds into a thousand shades of reds and oranges and colors known only to the heavens. Sunrise at the North Pole is not words, it is music; a song sung but once a year in perfect harmony with every universe, known and unknown. Not a sight to be squandered, a sight to be applauded.

Home.

"Good to be home," he called to the singing angels.

But for how long?

CHAPTER FIFTY-FIVE

ROGER

SNOW. MORE SNOW THAN DONNA WORTHY HAD EVER SEEN. IF SHE opened her bedroom window, she could reach outside and touch the top of a snowdrift. It didn't feel like being in a cave after all. It felt like being on top of the clouds. She thought about crawling out the window and making a Butterfly angel so she could look at it every night at bedtime and pretend that Butterfly was right there outside her window. She stared at the snowdrift, imagining a Butterfly angel, imagining Butterfly, imagining ... someone shoveling snow?

She leaned out the window as far as she could without falling, but the snow was too high to see over.

"Mom?" Donna called.

It was cold outside. She could see her breath and wondered if the little cloud of frozen air meant *Mom* in some kind of winter language.

"Mom?" she called a little louder. This time her frozen breath looked different. Oh well.

"Are you okay?" she heard her mom ask from the doorway behind her. "And why are you halfway out the window? It's *cold* out there!"

"I thought you were shoveling the snow. Listen."

Danni Worthy moved from her daughter's bedroom door to her window, leaned out and ...

"Who in the world? No! It can't be! Close your window and stay in your room!"

Danni charged from the room to the front door, flung it open it and jumped outside into the cold, wrapping her terrycloth robe tightly around her. The first thing she saw was the Santa hat.

"Stop! Nick! Santa! Whoever you are, you're not supposed to be here!"

The man in the Santa hat turned to look at Danni.

"Roger?"

His cheeks were as red as tomatoes and his eyelashes were coated with frost but his smile was wide and warming. He looked like he'd never been happier.

"Morning, Danni. Almost done."

"Roger, you're shoveling snow. What's gotten into you?"

"Christmas spirit, my dear, Christmas spirit has gotten into me!" He sounded as joyous and sincere as Scrooge, declaring, after a long night with the three ghosts of Christmas, *"I will honor Christmas in my heart, and try to keep it all the year. I will live in the Past, the Present, and the Future. The Spirits of all Three shall strive within me."*

"I don't get it."

"It's simple, my dear. When I saw the old fellow, the one in the Santa suit, shovel you out from under the last snowfall and then shovel *me* out and then go across the street and shovel *Mae Rose* out from under and then just walk away and not ask for anything, I thought to myself, that man, that *old* man, is just loaded with a giving spirit." He paused to take a breath. Danni pulled her robe even tighter around her, shuffled her feet up and down against the cold..

"So this morning, when I saw all this snow," he waved the shovel in an arc. It flipped out of his hands and landed at the bottom of Danni's steps. "Whoops. Anyway, and don't ask me why, I decided to shovel us out. *All* of us. And you know what, Danni? It felt good. *Feels* good."

"Wow, Roger. Wow, wow, wow!"

"Yes, wow indeed! *And* Mae Rose came out of her house carrying that scrawny old cat of hers and gave me a bowl of the best soup I've ever tasted. Win, win, my dear. Win, win!"

"Wait here, Roger," Danni said, holding one hand in the air. Minutes later she was back with a steaming mug of hot chocolate.

"Best I can do on short notice, Roger."

"Is this a reindeer ace on the mug?"

"Yeah. Looks kinda like Cupid, don't you think?"

"I wouldn't know. I've never met the man."

CHAPTER FIFTY-SIX

LETTERS FROM SANTA

Dear Betsy,

You told me that you consider the men you serve to be lost lambs that have found their way to St. Patrick's Haven. "Lost and lonely lambs" I believe you said. One of your lambs, a young man named Daniel, is indeed lost and lonely. You will find him in the Mental Health Unit at the hospital. Perhaps you could make a call to someone who can arrange to have Daniel moved to where he will be safe and be able to get the help he needs?

Thank you and Merry Christmas.

Nick

~

Detective Popporicht,

I will not be pressing any charges against the young man you are holding in the Mental Health Unit. When someone shows up to take him to where he will be safe and get the help he needs, please do not stand in the way of doing the right thing.

Thank you and Merry Christmas.

Just Nick.

CHAPTER FIFTY-SEVEN

THE RED BOX

BEFORE GOING DOWN TO THE WORKSHOP, SANTA TOOK A MOMENT TO stand in front of the Scotch Pine and breathe in the walk in the forest. Mrs. came up behind him, wrapped her arms around his middle.

"Did you notice?" she asked.

"Notice?"

"Look under the tree."

Grodan's gift, the little red box, was gone.

"Interesting," Santa said, looking at the empty spot beneath the tree where the little red box had been. "It has gone to a fisherman."

PROFESSOR MATHIAS PEDERSEN sat at his usual table in the Einstein Cafe & bel étage, studying the little red box, rolling it over and over in his hands, like it was a Rubik's Cube, a mystery needing to be solved. He had found it in his mailbox. A Christmas gift from one of his students, perhaps? He looked at his watch. One minute before the clock would strike. Time enough to open such a small box.

Inside the red box was a mirror. He held it up to his face.

The clock struck. The crowd outside cheered.

The professor heard none of it as he rushed from the cafe, clutching the mirror like it was made of gold, giggling like a child, hugging everyone in his path, telling them, "Fish! Yes, fish! I love fish!"

CHAPTER FIFTY-EIGHT

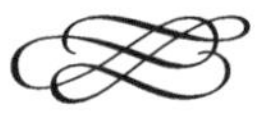

THE FIRST KISS

When he was eight-years old and in the third grade, Mathias Pedersen kissed Mia Hille full on her lips in the school cafeteria. It was his first kiss. Mia responded by dumping a bowl of green pea soup with bacon and cod over his head. He didn't care. It was a first kiss. A stolen kiss. The feeling was dizzying.

More than fifty years later, Professor Mathias Pedersen opened a little red box, looked into a mirror and saw what had been staring him in the face for months. The feeling was dizzying. First kiss dizzying. Stolen kiss dizzying.

He had long suspected that the origins of ALPINE Virus would eventually be traced back to a fish. There was a paper on his desk, a veterinary research paper he had put aside to read later. Put aside every morning for the past three weeks. He picked it up. Began to read.

. . .

Fish possess numerous distinct and complex defense mechanisms to protect themselves from pathogenic infections ... fish skin mucus acts as the first line of physical defense ... certain proteins found in the mucus of the Atlantic Cod create an innate immunity to certain bacteria.

Reading between the lines, the professor drew his own conclusion ... if a fish could be the origin of a virus, could not a fish also be the antidote?

The next morning, Professor Mathias Pedersen was on his way to the most beautiful place in the world.

He was going fishing.

CHAPTER FIFTY-NINE

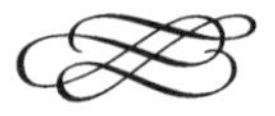

THE INVISIBLE MAN

SANTA HAD BEEN DISAPPEARING, FADING IN AND OUT OF WHEREVER HE was like a reluctant ghost weighing its options between the here and the hereafter.

In the kitchen, while Mrs. was shooing Santa away from a fresh baked dozen of his favorite oatmeal raisin cookies, he disappeared only to reappear a few seconds later, unaware of what had happened. In the workshop, with Grodan, Santa disappeared and then reappeared some seconds later, unaware of what had happened. Once, standing alone on an ice floe, listening to the angels sing, he disappeared for more than an hour.

For two days, he was there and then he wasn't.

Disappearing.

Like a Skipper.

When Mrs. and Grodan told him what was happening, Santa assured them both that he was not doing it on his own. But as he kept disappearing more and more for longer and longer lengths of time, he realized ...

"He 's moving!"

"Who's moving, Santa?" Mrs. and Grodan both asked.

"God is moving. When He told me I had to return to Erie and I asked Him how would I know when I would be returning, He said, *"You'll know."*

Santa disappeared again.

This time, he did not return.

CHAPTER SIXTY

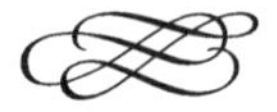

THE MALL

Seven days before Christmas.

"The job pays forty dollars an hour, fifty if you speak two languages, even more if you can sign with the hearing impaired. We prefer you don't smoke, we insist you do not drink alcohol, use drugs, raise your voice, use foul language and do not lose your temper if one of the little ones screams, bursts into tears, yanks on your beard, hits you or accidentally pees while sitting on your lap. Contrary to what most parents think, this can be a traumatic experience for a child."

His name was Martin, a short, important-looking man in a gray suit, dull blue shirt and red tie. Even though he looked to be only thirty something, his hair was already white, already thinning. His eyes were the same dull blue as his shirt. He was so full of nervous energy that he rocked back and forth on the balls of his feet, probably unaware that he was doing it. When he talked, every word sounded clipped, like he was talking in shorthand. Maybe because it looked like he had no lips. At the moment, he was talking to Santa Claus who stood, in a daze, looking all around. Minutes ago he was at the North Pole with Mrs. and Grodan and now, minutes later, here he was, in the mall where it had all begun only two short weeks ago, standing next to a man who seemed to know him.

"Hey! Hey!" Martin was on his tip toes snapping his fingers in Santa's face. "Stay with me, here, big fella, this is important." A look of concern suddenly came over his face. "Wait a minute! Wait just a minute here! Look at me!" Santa looked at him. Martin moved his own face within inches of Santa's, so close Santa could smell onion rings on his breath. He whispered, "Are you on something?"

"I don't know what that means," Santa whispered back.

Martin studied him a full minute before nodding and stepping back.

"Always stay in character, " Martin continued. "Do not use the public restrooms, do not eat onion, garlic or other foul smelling foods, brush your beard before every shift, do not make any promises to any child or parent, be a good listener, talk as little as possible and do not even flinch if a child rubs anything gooey over your coat. So ... are you up to the job?"

"Job?" Santa asked, still looking around.

"Yes, job! Who shows up at a mall looking like Santa Claus if not someone looking for a job *as* Santa Claus?"

"You want me to be Santa Claus? In your mall?"

"I won't lie to you, big fella, this weather, all these storms, we've been hit hard in the Santa department. I think we have one left. The others have either quit or not shown up. You look the part and I need you."

"But ..." Santa stopped himself, remembering ...

"The child needs you."

"But I failed her. I failed You. How can I be of any use to anyone anymore?"

"Be who you are."

He looked at Martin, rocking back and forth on his heels, fidgeting with his tie.

"Yes, I'll be Santa Claus in your mall. When would you like me to start?"

"Look behind you."

A line of children stretched all the way back to the mall entrance.

Santa stepped up to the green velvet throne, took a seat and held out his arms.

Martin jumped aside as the first child rushed toward the throne. "What's your name? I'll need it for my records."

"I'm Santa Claus."

"Staying in character. I like that."

CHAPTER SIXTY-ONE

DEAR SANTA

THE CHILDREN CAME TO SEE SANTA, ONE BY ONE BY ONE ...

Logan. Age 6: *I would like a pony and some land to ride it on.*

Noah. Age 7: *How did you get my bike down the chimney last year?*

Mia. Age 7: *I don't feel like talking but I made a list.*

Ava. Age 8: *Uncle Ralph says to tell you he wants a redhead.*

Jacob. Age 5: *The cookies are in that round, white thing in the kitchen. Take as many as you want but leave a note telling mom it was you and not me.*

Penny. Age 7: *I was an elf in the play. When all of us elfs walked on stage our elf hats kept on falling off. How do your elfs keep their hats on tight?*

Madison. Age 5: *I thought you'd like to know that I'll be living real close to you soon because we've moving to Michigan.*

Ethan. Age 6: *I'm practicing staying up late so I'll be awake when you come.*

Oliver. Age 8: *We don't have a chimney so bring one of your elfs to climb down our stove pipe and unlock the door for you.*

Isabella. Age 7: *All I want for Christmas is for mom to be happy. She wants to have another baby but she can't.*

Olivia. Age 5: *Can the reindeers talk?*

Dylan. Age 4: *Oops.*

Anthony. Age 6: *Can you bring my grammy a washing machine? She don't get around so good no more and the laundrymat is too far away.*

Lunch break. Santa had visited with forty-three children and posed for photos with forty-one of them. A curly-haired girl named Lucy, who couldn't stop sneezing and Lance, a redheaded boy who shouted to his red-faced mother, "Okay, I did it! Where are my chicken nuggets?" declined the photo op. There were also three elderly ladies who had a group photo taken with the old saint.

"It's for this year's Christmas card" the one called Meryl said, raising her finger and, on cue, all three ladies sang out, "*Believing never gets old!*"

CHAPTER SIXTY-TWO

THE FOOD COURT

MARTIN HAD GIVEN SANTA SEVERAL VOUCHERS, "HONORED AT ANY OF the fine eateries in our food court." It was more of an assurance policy than an act of kindness or Christmas spirit. Martin needed to be assured that his Santas never left the mall during their shift. Giving them free meals at the food court was better than having them wander off campus on their breaks and not return or, worse, wander off campus and return "out of character". He still had nightmares about the Santa who had left the mall on his break and come back with a quart of "special" egg nog which he sipped between visits with the children. He'd been back on the job an hour when he rose unsteadily from the throne, wished everyone a very Happy Easter and passed out standing up.

Santa had eaten at the food court only one other time, with Lenny Schwartz. Philly Cheesesteaks from Charleys. They'd been good enough then that he'd gone back for more today. Before he took his first bite, he couldn't help but think of Lenny and smile and say, "If this right here ain't a piece of art, it's ..."

"... a work of art!"

"Lenny?"

"Livin' an' breathin', Santa." Lenny said with a sly grin as he slid into the chair opposite Santa. "Or should I say Nick?"

Santa smiled.

"I *knew* it!" Lenny fist pumped the air between them and then leaned back and studied Santa like he might study the cover of a book, trying to decide whether or not he should read it.

"You ain't the only one changed," he said quietly, seriously.

"Changed?"

"Remember what you said last time I saw you, about lookin' in the mirror? Any time I look in the mirror all I ever see is this guy, the Bogeyman, halfway through his life with nothin' to show for it but ugly. Then you said what you said an' ... well, I got a story to tell ya. Are you stayin' at the Haven tonight?"

Santa blinked. He hadn't known he'd be here, at the mall, had no idea how long he was *going* to be here, had not thought about a place to stay, so ...

"Yes, I guess I am."

"I'll see ya there." Lenny stood, closed his eyes, touched his finger to his nose and pushed.

"Am I still here?" Lenny asked, his eyes still squeezed shut.

"Yes." answered Santa.

"It was worth a shot."

CHAPTER SIXTY-THREE

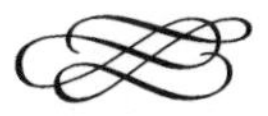

ST. PATRICK'S HAVEN

SANTA WAS HOPING TO SEE BETSY BUZZING AROUND ST. PATRICK'S Haven, giving out bananas and apples and words of encouragement but she was at a fund-raiser dinner and not expected back till the following day. He'd have to wait till then to learn whether or not she'd been able to help get Daniel out of the Mental Health Unit and into a safe place.

He'd left the mall shortly after five to register for a bed at St. Patrick's Haven and then returned to the mall to use one of his food court vouchers, this time at Red Lobster where he lingered over clam chowder and Cheddar Bay biscuits until St. Patrick's opened its doors promptly at seven-thirty. "Martin would approve," Santa murmured to himself as he went looking for Lenny Schwartz. He found him by the coffee corner, spooning sugar into a mug of hot coffee.

They found a quiet corner, the same quiet corner Santa had found the night he read *All About Butterflies.*

Lenny launched into his story.

"So there's this woman they call the Pear Lady. You don't know her but she was the one who wrapped her sweater around your head the night you got beat up. I'm not sayin' she saved your life but hey, just sayin'. Anyway she's as homeless as the rest of us but she sells pears on the street to make a buck or two, y'know? So, we're at the Tim Horton's a couple days ago talkin' and she tells me her real name is Lois an' she's from Kentucky, which I kinda figured 'cause she's got one of them voices that sound like it's singin' lullabies. Before she went street, she was one 'a them care people, you know, takin' care 'a sick people, until one of them died in her arms while she was tryin' to sing them to sleep. Broke her heart so bad she couldn't do it no more, stopped workin', stopped singin', spent the last few bucks she had to get as far away from Kentucky as she could, ended up here, sellin' pears on the street."

Lenny went quiet, swallowed hard, picked up his story.

"I told her she got it all wrong, like if it was my turn to meet my Maker an' I had a choice of listenin' to her sing me into heaven or me just dyin' on my own, I'd take her every time. Then I told her that the guy she was helpin' in front of the Tim Horton's was a friend 'a mine and he didn't die an' she helped with that an' she should do what you told me to do the night I saw you writin' them notes."

"See who you are and be who you are." Santa said softly.

"Right. I told her that. I said, 'Hey, go look in a mirror. You ain't the Pear Lady, you're the Care Lady, Lois from Kentucky.'"

"Did she?"

"I dunno but I ain't seen her since. Hey, it's Christmas time. Miracles happen, right?"

"All the time."

"So, maybe there's somethin' to this look in the mirror stuff?"

"Have you looked in the mirror?"

"Not yet."

CHAPTER SIXTY-FOUR

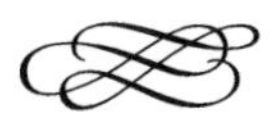

THE MALL

Six days before Christmas.

Darren. Age 8: *Come to my house first. I'm your biggest fan.*

Mary Ruth. Age 11: *I hope you don't mind me calling you by your first name Santa but I feel like I've known you all my life.*

Elizabeth. Age 5: *I always wondered what you looked like in person.*

Conrad. Age 6: *We'll leave the lights on for you. Please turn them off when you're finished.*

Chuck. Age 9: *I know some people that don't believe in you.*

Lynda. Age 9: *Could you come to my house a day earlier?*

Gerald. Age 7: *I have always wanted to meet you but I'm not allowed to stay up that late.*

Brian. Age 8: *You don't have to bring anything to Barry. He has been very bad.*

Heather. Age 9: *Did you know there are Christmas angels? They work for God to watch over kids when God has to go do something else.*

Mason. Age 6: *I don't need any more clothes.*

It was just before five. Santa was brushing potato chips from his throne. A voice called from behind.

"Got time for two more, Santa?"

Santa turned to see Danni Worthy and her daughter, Donna, approaching the throne.

CHAPTER SIXTY-FIVE

THE JOURNEY

"DO YOU EVER GET LETTERS FROM KIDS IN HEAVEN?"

Donna sat next to Santa on his throne. It didn't look like a throne. It looked like a green velvet love seat, big enough to hold Santa and at least two more people. Little people. Like Donna Worthy, who sat quietly staring at her red winter boots, waiting for an answer.

"No, I don't."

"Have you ever seen heaven?"

"Yes, I have."

"Have you seen the kids that are there?"

He never had but he knew heaven to be full of children, lifted from their parents' arms into the arms of an angel. Forever safe in a place where moonbeams tap at their windows, inviting them out to play; a place where they can go riding on cloud-covered ponies through star-studded skies, just by thinking it and every star a wishing star; a place where they can gather in a circle and listen to Lewis Carroll read to them not only of Alice's adventures in a place called Wonderland but also of new adventures Mr. Carroll has written since his arrival into heaven. Frances Hodgson Burnett will not only read to the children from her book, *The Magic Garden*, but have them close their eyes and join her in the garden for tea; the writers of *Peter Pan, Winnie the Pooh, The Velveteen Rabbit* and so many others are there, waiting to entertain heaven's children.

Heaven is full of children, forever at play, forever young, forever alive. A place where they close their eyes and sleep, in heavenly peace, to dream and wait for those they left behind.

Santa knew all of this but he had never seen any of it.

"I've never seen the children in heaven," he said to Donna. "But I've heard them laughing."

"Do you think you heard my sister? Her real name is Amber but we called her Butterfly and she squeaks when she laughs. Real loud."

Donna looked away from Santa, swinging her legs, thumping her red-booted feet against the green velvet throne awhile before she said, almost whispered, without looking up, "It's my fault she died. I'm older than her and it should have been me who had the skin disease and I should have been the one who had to wear the bandages and ...."

“Child,” Santa said, in a voice as soft as air, “no one can decide who gets sick and who doesn't.”

“God can.”

A gentle quiet settled over Santa's throne. Donna looked into Santa's eyes. Waiting. Santa took Donna's hands in his and said, "I'm going to tell you about a journey."

Santa thought back to what God had told him.

The journey of the soul is filled with everything imaginable and everything unimaginable, everything expected and everything unexpected; everything we hope will happen and everything we hope will never happen. Welcome it all like you would welcome a friend. Welcome the joy, the love, the sadness, the sorrow, the intimacy, the ecstasy like you would welcome the dawn. Welcome the dreams, the hopes, the pain, the loss, the emptiness, the fullness, the richness like you would welcome a warm place by the fire. Welcome everything like a child would welcome a mother's arms, knowing that every time you stumble, you have stumbled onto a stepping stone on a journey that will lead you home.

"But how do I explain all that to a seven-year-old?" Santa wondered.

He took a deep breath, let it out ever so slowly and began ... "God sends everyone on a journey. It is called the Journey of the Soul because, even when we get so sick it makes us die, we have something that never dies. A soul."

"Do kids have a soul?"

"They do. It's that part of you that feels good inside when your mother's hair tickles your face when she kisses you goodnight. It's that part of you that made you laugh at your sister's butterfly tricks and, it's that part of you that feels sad when you think of her now.

"No one knows how long and how far their soul will journey through the world. Some journeys seem too short, like Butterfly's journey, but not for her. She was on a journey of courage and strength. Her journey hurt every step of the way but she kept going until her journey here ended but did not end here. She is not gone, child. She has gone on to continue her journey in a place without pain.

"Can I go see her?"

"You can not go where she is Donna, but she can go where you are. You can carry her with you everywhere you go so that whenever you need some extra courage and strength all you have to do is call on her and she will bring it to you."

He squeezed her hands. "It's no one's fault when someone dies. It's just the end of this part of their journey."

Danni Worthy stepped forward. "Hey, you two, you're sure taking a long time to talk about Christmas presents. It's my turn." She held up a piece of paper. "I have a list."

"Ahem." It was Martin, stepping out from behind the pillar. "I'm sorry, madam, but it is now several *minutes* past closing time for Santa and we do not allow overtime. If you'll come back tomorrow at a scheduled hour, I'm sure the jolly old saint will be happy to accommodate you and your list."

To emphasize his point he flicked a switch on the throne killing all the lights.

Donna Worthy hopped from Santa's throne and stood looking at the old saint, studying him the way one might study a photograph of a long lost friend. She smiled, reached up and touched his beard and said, “I always knew you were real.”

CHAPTER SIXTY-SIX

DONNA'S LIST

NOT LONG AFTERWARD DONNA WORTHY FELT HER MOTHER'S HAIR tickle her face as she leaned down to kiss her goodnight.

"Mom, do you know what a soul is?"

"I think so. Why? Where did you ...?"

"Do you think your soul is different than mine?"

"I think so."

"What makes your soul feel good?"

Without missing a beat, Danni Worthy took her daughter's hands in her own and whispered, "You make my soul feel good."

She smiled, leaned down and kissed her again, then stood and walked softly from the room.

When she was gone, Donna leaned over the side of her bed, reached under it and pulled out her box of colored pens and a sketch pad. She turned to a clean sheet of paper and began to draw. When she was done, the picture looked like all the others in the sketch pad. Pictures she had drawn every night since Butterfly died. Pictures of a girl. A girl with wings. Butterfly wings. On this night though, beneath the girl in the picture, was a list:

Nothing scared her

Her squeaky laugh made me laugh out loud

She was very brave

She never cried

She liked butterflies

The look on her face when I read to her about a girl who could fly

Donna felt like *she* could fly. Was it her soul that made her feel like that?

Or was it what Santa Claus had whispered to her as they said goodbye at the mall?

"It's a gift. Life is a gift and gifts are for giving. Butterfly's life was a gift to you from her. When you go home, write down all the things you love about her gift - all the things no one can ever take away and that you can never forget. And then write one word that says how you feel about having Butterfly in your life - Butterfly the gift."

The only word Donna could think of was "Lucky".

A FEW MILES AWAY, Santa sat on one of the bottom bunks in St. Patrick's Haven. He still hadn't seen Betsy but really, was that why he was still in Erie, Pennsylvania? The only word that came to mind was, "Unfinished".

CHAPTER SIXTY-SEVEN

THE MALL

FIVE DAYS BEFORE CHRISTMAS.

Santa arrived at the mall early. Martin was waiting for him.

"I won't be needing you after today. Most of my regular Santas have surfaced and I did promise them a full season, so I'm sure you understand. I will say, however, that aside from your penchant for spending an inordinate amount of time with the children, you have done an admirable job. Saved the day, in fact, and there will be a nice bonus added to your check." He waved his hand in the air, like he was swatting at a mosquito. "No need to thank me. You earned it. Which reminds me, please drop by the office on your break and give them all the pertinent payroll information. One of my staff will bring your check to you before five today. Five o'clock sharp. Quitting time."

He nodded his head sharply, like a punctuation mark, rocked back and forth on his heels once and then turned and moved quickly into the mall, like a man with important things to do, nearly colliding with a group of morning mall walkers.

Santa watched Martin until he disappeared down the hallway leading to his office.

"What do you do on Christmas Day, Martin?" he wondered aloud. "Do you have family? Do you have friends? Do you take your tie off? Is there more to your life than this place? I hope so. Or do you rock back and forth until Christmas is over and then rush back to work? I hope not. Do you ..."

"It's *you*, isn't it?"

Santa turned, startled at the sound of the voice. Danni Worthy stood just a few feet away, her shoulders hunched forward, her hands deep in the pockets of her parka, her eyes locked onto the old saint's face.

"Nick, Santa, whoever. I don 't know *how* it's you, but it's you."

She did not sound like the happy-go-lucky woman who had teased him about being Santa on a bad hair day. She did not look like the strong, confident woman he had sat with on the porch only days ago while she poured out her heart. She looked ... defeated.

"Do you hate me?" she asked.

"I don't know what that means."

She shrugged. "'Course you don't, you're Santa Claus. What does Santa Claus know about hate?" She took her hands out of her pockets, something crumpled in each one. "I had you arrested and then that detective, the one they call Pop, came by and told me someone had hurt you so bad you almost died but you weren't going to press charges and then you disappeared. He said maybe you really are a good guy and maybe he was wrong about you and he gave me these letters." She opened both hands. "From Donna to Santa, you, Nick, whoever you are.

"I thought you were gone for good. but then yesterday ..." She took a breath. "Yesterday you spent all that time with Donna and when she told me what you told her about the Journey of the Soul and about the children in heaven and about life being a gift we give to others, I knew it was you and I knew you were who I thought you were the day I met you. Someone good."

The tears came. She didn't try to stop them.

"Whether it's true or if you made it all up, it doesn't matter because it worked! Donna sees Butterfly in a safe and happy place, *believes* she's in a safe and happy place and most important of all, she doesn't blame herself anymore for what happened. Because of you, I have my daughter back and I came here to say thank you and tell you how sorry I am for all the hurt I have caused you."

She stood looking at the old saint for a full minute. Neither of them said anything. She mumbled another, "I'm sorry." and turned to go.

"Would you like some hot chocolate? I have vouchers."

Still with her back to him, Danni Worthy blurted out a laugh and said, "Yes. I would love some hot chocolate." She turned to face him, wiping the tears from her eyes with the back of her hand. "And I have cookies!" She reached into her pocket and pulled out a plastic baggy with four oatmeal raisin cookies inside.

DANNI WENT for the hot chocolate while Santa visited with the children already lining up to meet with him and share their secret wishes.

Debbie. Age 8: *Can I have your phone number? I promise I won't call unless it's an emergency.*

Cindy. Age 6: *I try to be good, Santa, but it's very hard when I have three brothers bugging me all the time.*

Hanson. Age 9: *If you give me more toys than my brother, I won 't tell him you're not real.*

Danni sat on a chair a few feet from the green velvet throne, marveling at the patience, the gentleness, the love that poured forth from this man who was or was not Santa Claus and again felt the sting of tears of guilt well in her eyes. "I'm sorry," she whispered again. She wanted him to be real because, if he really was Santa Claus, she would give him her annual list of things she wanted God to change in the world. Who knows? If he *was* Santa Claus, he might even have God's address?

Martin came by twice, but if he noticed Danni sitting near the throne he likely assumed she was a mother waiting for her child. The second time he came by, he tapped Santa on the shoulder and reminded him, in a low voice, "Don't forget. My office, on your break." Whatever that meant.

~

BREAK TIME.

They ate Philly cheesesteaks from Charleys.

"My friend, Lenny Schwartz, calls these sandwiches a work of art and I have to agree with him."

Danni took a bite.

"Wow! Your friend, Lenny Schwartz, knows his sandwiches!"

She took another bite. "Wanna hear a Christmas miracle, Nick? Santa?"

Santa nodded his head.

"Roger shoveled us out from under the last storm."

Santa swallowed. "*Roger* did that?"

"He said he was inspired by you. *And* he shoveled Mae Rose out from under. She gave him some soup."

Santa smiled, nodded his head, thought of Franklin, God rest his soul.

"I'd put a bowl of my soup down in front of him and he would look at me every time like I was the queen of the world and he would eat my soup every time like he was the king of the world."

Santa smiled again.

"Joe's really sick. " Danni said. She sounded scared.

Santa looked at her. Waited.

"He has something called ALPINE Virus. We thought he had picked up some kind of bug at work, but the other day I found him lying on the bedroom floor, unconscious. We got him to the hospital and they did tests and figured it was this new virus.

She took a breath. "People are dying from it."

Danni looked across the food court, not at anyone or anything, just ... out there, where she could get her emotions under control. She turned her eyes on Santa.

"I lost a daughter. I can't lose my husband."

Santa took her hand in his. Squeezed. "Don't lose faith. There's an answer. There always is."

She gave him a weak smile. "They told me there's a professor Pedersen in Switzerland who's working on an antidote. Maybe we'll have another miracle? Like Roger shoveling snow."

"Pedersen?" Santa raised his eyebrows and returned her smile. "Maybe we will."

She stood. "Gotta go. Thank you for the sandwich, thank you for the hot chocolate, thank you for ... everything." She held out her hand. "And we're good, right?'

"Almost."

"Almost?"

"You haven't told me what you want for Christmas."

She smiled a mischievous smile.

"Surprise me."

AT FIVE O'CLOCK SHARP that evening, Santa turned off the lights that surrounded the green velvet throne, put his finger to his nose, imagined himself back home and went there.

CHAPTER SIXTY-EIGHT

SURPRISE

FOUR DAYS BEFORE CHRISTMAS.

Butterfly had died. Danni had fought for her daughter's life, would have given her own life if it meant Butterfly would live. But all the hoping and praying and begging and bargaining led only to tears, anger, guilt, brokenness, questions and dreams of what might have been. Danni Worthy was helpless to save her daughter.

Donna Worthy took it especially hard. Danni tried everything and would have given anything to spare her only other child the pain of a loss that came too, too soon in her young life. Donna disappeared within herself, became quiet, moody, aloof, blaming herself for Butterfly's death and no matter how hard Danni hoped and prayed and begged and bargained, she was helpless to save her daughter.

Joe Worthy was sick. Maybe dying. Again Danni hoped and prayed and begged and bargained but again, she was helpless to save her husband.

Her life was spinning out of control. She was hanging on by a thread and no matter how hard she hoped and prayed and begged and bargained, the thread was unraveling and Danni was falling, falling, falling into a place as empty as an abandoned house.

And then came this man, Nick, Santa, whoever he was; a man so full of goodness and giving how could there be room left inside him for anything more? A man who made children laugh and dance and believe in the impossible and, if they would open their minds, a man who taught fathers and mothers and all the others how to dance to the music of the child in their heart.

"Don't lose faith. There's an answer. There always is." Santa told her.

For the first time in months, Danni believed it.

What did she want for Christmas?

She wanted miracles and lots of them. Roger shoveling snow kinds of miracles.

"MAIL'S EARLY TODAY," she said to no one in particular, pulling the envelope from the box.

Details on the check inside the envelope included: 3 *days seasonal employment @ $400/day; $500 seasonal bonus;* After standard deductions, the net amount of the check was $1484.95. It was Santa's paycheck, made payable to Danielle Worthy.

Surprise!

Danni's voice croaked as she laughed and sang into the morning, "Nick, Santa, whoever you are, I love you!" She looked again at the check. "For three day's work? I need to buy a beard and let my hair grow out!"

She did not notice that her entire front yard was covered in angels. Butterfly angels.

CHAPTER SIXTY-NINE

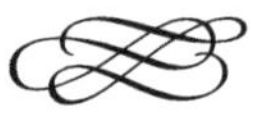

REINE, NORWAY

"Have you found him, Grodan?"

"Yes, Santa, he is in Reine, Norway, gathering fish.""

Santa gave a quick wave to Grodan and Mrs., put his finger to his nose, saw himself in Reine, Norway, and went there.

Mathias Pedersen was born in the most beautiful place in the world - the tiny fishing village of Reine on the island of Moskenesøya on northern Norway's Lofoten archipelago. It's on the map but just barely and the three hundred or so weathered souls calling Reine their home are okay with that.

The only son of a single-minded fisherman, Mathias was christened into the family business almost before he could walk when his father deliberately stuck a needlepoint hook into the palm of his son's right hand and then just as deliberately yanked it out.

"Fishing is in the blood," his father told him, letting the boy's palm bleed while he strung the hook onto a piece of fishing line and hung it around Mathias' neck.

"Respect the fish. Honor the fish. The fish is your life, Mathias. You will see."

His life. Casting nets, dragging nets, hauling nets, emptying nets. Killing, filleting, gutting and freezing; cruel, biting winds, high seas, rogue waves, suffocating salt water; cold, dark, deafening and always just one step away from being swallowed up by the sea.

Fishing.

He hated it. Hated fish.

Two weeks after Mathias turned seventeen his mother succumbed to a then unidentified strain of pneumonia. He stood at her graveside in the shadow of the Reinefjorden and promised her he would dedicate his life not to fish, but to ridding the world of infectious disease. If there was a heaven (he was going to be a scientist, he would need proof) he knew his mother would be in it. He knew she would be pleased with his graveside promise and he knew it would not smell like fish.

He hated fish.

At age nineteen, Mathias was accepted into the University of Bern, nearly two thousand miles away. He turned his back on the most beautiful place in the world and spent the next forty years immersed in immunology, the study of the human body's defense system, leaning toward the study of infectious diseases and therapies related to the treatment of those diseases.

And now he was back, fishing for the antidote to ALPINE Virus.

And Santa Claus, known as Julenissen in Norway, was knocking at his door.

"Hold on, I am here," a voice that sounded like it had been stretched through time called from inside, followed by a slow thump, thump, thump and a series of painful grunts. The door opened. The strong odor of raw fish pushed it's way past the old man standing in the doorway.

He was tall and thin, in his late seventies with a face so weather worn and wrinkled he could have been ten years younger or ten years older. Most of his face was hidden behind a thick white beard. A mustache hung over his mouth like a shag rug hanging over a clothesline. He had a nose like an onion bulb, hair like an Old English Sheepdog and tired steel gray eyes that had stared down too many ocean storms. He leaned heavily to his right, balancing himself on a homemade crutch.

"What does Julenissen want with me?" he asked.

"Mathias?"

"I am Noah. Mathias is my son. What does Julenissen want with my son?"

"I would like to speak with him," Santa peered over the old man's slumped shoulders, squinting into the darkness. He could see there was a fire in the fireplace but beyond that, nothing. "Is he home?"

Noah chinned his head back and pointed over Santa's shoulder. "He is at the water. Every day at the water, buying more fish. All of his life, he hates fish and now he can not stop buying fish."

"How will I know him."

"He will be the one who does not look like a fisherman." The elder Pedersen shook his wooly head, bunny-hopped one step backwards on his crutch and closed the door. Santa began to work his way down the path that led to the harbor, getting the attention of three locals standing outside the old white wooden church that had been standing in Reine for over one hundred years.

"Julenissen," called one of the three, a hard-faced man holding his hands in prayer. "I am praying that you fill my socks with gold this year. I need a new engine in my boat!"

"God dag, Julenissen," called another of the three, clenching a mariner's pipe between his teeth. "Bring me good luck."

The third, an older, red-cheeked woman who looked as though she had spent the best years of her life standing on the docks waiting for her ship to come in, laughed and said, "Julenissen, come sail away with me!"

Santa smiled and waved at the three of them and continued on toward the shore.

The bay was as still as ice and just as cold. A few loons scudded silently over the water, kicking up tiny ripples that set a couple of boats in motion, bobbing up and down as if nodding to each other in agreement that what Santa had come here to do was the right thing to do.

The only thing to do.

CHAPTER SEVENTY

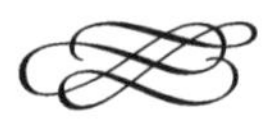

THE ANTIDOTE

THE ONLY MAN WHO DID NOT LOOK LIKE A FISHERMAN, A MAN STUFFING large fish into a larger bucket, knelt on the shore shooing away a white-tailed eagle while it krick-krick-kricked at him, begging him to leave just one of his fish behind.

"Gå vekk! Catch your own, bird. These are for science! Gå vekk!"

"Hello, Mathias."

The professor looked up, startled, a fish still in his hands. Smiled at what he saw.

"Julenissen! What brings the Christmas elf out of hiding?"

"You do, Mathias. You and your fish."

The professor cocked his head to one side, looked at his bucket of fish, looked back at Santa.

"What does Julenissen want with my fish?"

"The antidote to ALPINE Virus. You figured it out, didn't you?"

Mathias Pedersen stood, let the fish drop from his hands. The eagle swooped in, grabbed the fish and was gone.

"Who are you?"

"You call me Julenissen."

"A figment! A child's fantasy!" The professor pointed a finger at Santa and demanded to know, "Who are you?"

"When you were a boy, you sent me a letter telling me your dog had run away. We found your dog and brought it home to you."

"Anyone could know that. It is a small village and you ..."

"You said it was the best dog in all of Norway because it hated fish."

Mathias couldn't help but smile at the memory.

"Yes," he said, still smiling, "that was a smart dog. Everyone in the village knew it." He picked up his bucket of fish, moved toward Santa. "Thank you for the memory, Julenissen, but I have no more time for gossip."

He shouldered his way around the old saint and started up the hill toward his father's house.

"The red box," Santa called after him.

The professor stiffened, like he had been turned to stone.

Santa continued. "You received a small red box. Inside was a mirror and when you looked into the mirror, you saw the answer to your question."

"Fish," the professor said, raising the bucket of fish into the air. He turned to face Santa. "The answer is fish. Skin mucus from the Atlantic Cod. The missing element. *You* gave me the red box?"

"No. The red box is a gift of providence, given to someone different every year."

"I am a scientist. You are a myth. Providence is a ..." he struggled for a word, flipping his hand back and forth. " ... a concept. This is all very hard for me to accept as fact."

"And yet here you stand, with a bucket of fish, taking providence at its word, talking to a myth. Have you developed the antidote?"

The professor hesitated before nodding his head. "I have. I will be returning home tomorrow to begin testing on a group of volunteers."

"Will it work?"

"Without a doubt."

"I have one more volunteer for you."

CHAPTER SEVENTY-ONE

ORANGES

THREE DAYS BEFORE CHRISTMAS.

"Oranges?" Joe's voice was weak, raspy.

"Baby mandarins," Danni said. "My mother used to call them Japanese oranges. We had a box of them every Christmas. This box was on the porch this morning, addressed to you. Very mysterious."

They were in Joe's hospital room. The box of oranges lay open on the bed. Danni plucked a note from the box.

Joe, eat two of the oranges today, two tomorrow morning and one each day after until the box is empty.

The note was not signed and there was no return address on the box.

TWO DAYS BEFORE CHRISTMAS.

Joe was sitting up in bed. He had eaten four of the oranges. ALPINE Virus was retreating from his body at a rate that was unexplainable.

"Rare," the doctors all admitted, scratching their heads. Easier that than having to admit they had no answer as to what in the world was happening.

CHAPTER SEVENTY-TWO

MIRACLES

Christmas Eve.

Joe was feeling strong enough to walk from one end of the hallway to the other and back again. No one asked why he insisted on carrying a box of oranges with him.

The doctors were still amazed and intrigued at the unexplainable turnaround in his condition. One of them suggested the best explanation was a "miracle" recovery. It was after all, almost Christmas.

"Kinda like Roger shoveling snow," Danni said. No one knew what that meant.

Danni and Donna hung four stockings on the end of Joe's hospital bed and stayed the night on rollaway beds brought in by the nurses.

Donna left three oatmeal raisin cookies and a glass of milk on the window sill.

CHAPTER SEVENTY-THREE

BUTTERFLY?

CHRISTMAS.

Danni found a mug in her stocking. A mug with a picture of a reindeer. Imprinted below the picture were the words, *This is Cupid.*

Joe found a book in his stocking - *All About Butterflies.*

Donna found a snow globe in her stocking. Inside the globe was a park bench. On the ground next to the bench was an angel. A Butterfly angel.

Butterfly's stocking had a flower in it. A purple flower.

All three oatmeal raisin cookies were gone and the glass of milk was empty.

DANNI AND JOE were talking quietly. Donna sat by the window, watching the icicles melt beneath a welcome warm winter sun, turning her snow globe over and over in her hands. Something moved, outside, at the bottom of the window. Donna lifted the window open a few inches. A butterfly fluttered into the room.

It was velvety brown with royal blue markings and wings trimmed in an off-white.

"Mom? Dad?"

Danni and Joe looked up. No one breathed. The butterfly hovered for a few seconds before flying over to light on Danni's face, next to a tear slowly winding its way down her cheek.

"Butterflies drink tears, Mom. The Santa Claus man in the park told me that."

The butterfly moved from Danni's face to flit back and forth in front of Joe, who blurted out, "Did a butterfly just flutter by?" The butterfly did a quick somersault and then flew to the open window, stopping to brush its wings against Donna's eyelashes. A butterfly kiss.

And then it was gone.

AS JOE FLIPPED the pages of *All About Butterflies* he noticed the author had dedicated a few pages to butterflies that stay through the winter.

"Among them," Joe read, "is the Mourning Cloak, a velvety brown, sometimes maroon-colored butterfly with royal blue markings and wings trimmed in an off-white. On warm winter days, it can be seen basking in the sun."

Leaving you, dear reader, to choose to believe what you believe.

CHAPTER SEVENTY-FOUR

LIFE GOES ON

PROFESSOR MATHIAS PEDERSEN RETURNED TO BERN WHERE HIS antidote was tested on one hundred volunteers and found to be one hundred percent effective, bringing an end to the nightmare that was ALPINE Virus. He and the man he knew as Julenissen, the Christmas Elf, had argued vigorously over how to get the antidote to Joe Worthy.

"You can not simply walk into a hospital room and inject a patient! The police will take you away like you are a madman!" the professor barked.

"It wouldn't be the first time," Santa countered.

"There are rules! Laws! Governments!"

"What if I wasn't there? What if Joe took the antidote on his own?"

That same night, Santa left a box of oranges on Danni Worthy's doorstep. Oranges injected with the antidote to ALPINE Virus.

ROGER GAVE UP SHOVELING SNOW. Inspiration can last only so long, but Roger did discover something within himself - a giving he never realized he had and ever since that Year of The Butterfly Christmas, he can look at the almost seven-foot tall man in the mirror and feel ... taller.

LENNY SCHWARTZ DISCOVERED he was good at convincing people to look beyond who they thought they were to see who they really are. He started with the homeless men he met at St. Patrick's Haven and before long, branched out to lecturing at homeless shelters across the state. Newspapers picked up on who and what he was and started writing about him. Eventually, a publishing house invited him to write a book.

"No problem. I'll call it *Invisible Me*."

They settled on *Be You*.

Within weeks of publication, Lenny received a copy of his book in the mail along with a note requesting he sign it - 'To the Care Lady' and return to sender. The return address was a small town in Kentucky.

BETSY DID CALL some people who called some people who got Daniel out of the Mental Health Unit and into a treatment center. His first giant step out of the darkness came the day he admitted to himself that even Al Capone, the gangster who started the first soup kitchen in Chicago, might actually have had at least an ounce of goodness in him.

TO THIS DAY, Betsy continues to be who she is - the woman who brings apples and bananas and hope to the homeless men of Erie. Every Christmas, she makes sure there are plenty of "blessing bags" for the men, stuffed with a hoodie, snacks, hand warmers and socks.

Her message never changes.

"St. Patrick's Haven was designed and built to accommodate homeless men of Erie and to be a place where their hope can be restored. Where they can know that they are people, too."

SANTA never again tried to be anyone but who he is, although, that Year of The Butterfly Christmas, the old saint came to realize that he was even more than he thought he was. He loved children, loved reading their letters, loved filling their stockings but, thanks to a man named Martin who had given him the joy of actually spending time with the children, it is rumored that for three days every Christmas, Santa chooses a mall somewhere in the world and takes a part-time job.

DANNI WORTHY still makes a Christmas list every year. But since The Butterfly Christmas it is no longer a list of all that is wrong in the world, it is a list of all that is right. She does not take the list to Santa. Instead she keeps it in her heart. She has finally found God's address.

And Donna Worthy?

CHAPTER SEVENTY-FIVE

ONE LAST LETTER

Dear Santa,

It's been fourteen years since The Butterfly Christmas! I still think of her every day and I still make Butterfly angels in the snow every chance I get. Sometimes I wonder if it was all just a dream. But then there have been times when I have needed a little extra courage and strength and I call on Butterfly. And you were right - she comes to the rescue every single time. I can't see her but I know she's there, invisible, like a Skipper, and in my heart I know she will always be with me and I will always be with her.

Your friend,

Donna Worthy

The End

ACKNOWLEDGMENTS

You write alone but you alone are not responsible for the outcome. This story could not have been complete nor completed without the help of a lot of good people. So, thank you - to Betsy Wiest, Executive Director, St. Patrick's Haven in Erie, PA for so much of your time and input; to Lenny Schwartz, who kindly lent his name and personality to one of the central characters in the story; to the people of the Special Services Division, United States Postal Service, Washington, DC for providing thousands of letters to Santa, among which were the two letters from the child I call Donna Worthy; to Wikipedia, for guiding me to hundreds of websites, ensuring that I got all the facts straight. Any that aren't straight are my fault. To Sam Severn, award-winning, NY Times best-selling ghostwriter, book doctor, screen-writer and writing coach for guiding me, word-by-word, through this entire story and finally, last but always first, to my own Donna. Who makes it all worthwhile.

ABOUT THE AUTHOR

William McDonald is an Emmy Award winning writer who, for more than 30 years, specialized in emotional communication in the broadcast industry. His documentary writing includes *The Elvis Presley Story, The Story of The Beatles, The Evolution of Rock,* audio books of several Turner Classic movies and the Christmas Special, *I'd Like to Wrap Up a Dream For You All* - all syndicated worldwide. He was a songwriter, director for the international touring group, *Up With People* and is the author of more than fifty Ebooks for Reading Town, NY. He spends several hours each week as a caregiver for senior men and writes full time from his home in Colorado.

Made in the USA
Las Vegas, NV
22 December 2022

63898240R00109